ABOVE THE SEA

LAURA BURTON
JESSIE CAL

BURTON & BURCHELL LTD

COPYRIGHT

Published by Burton & Burchell Ltd
To discuss rights: Laura@burtonburchell.co.uk

First Edition

Edited by Susie Poole
Cover Design: Wynter Designs

CHAPTER ONE

LEXA

*L*exa watched fireworks decorate the sky as she sat on a large rock at the edge of the ocean. Her wet, brown hair cascaded over two white seashells with gray speckles—the only form of clothing to keep her modesty. As was customary for mermaids.

She lowered her eyes to the poultice she mixed in a jar, using a stick, as she had done countless times before.

Hackett, a seagull and friend, landed on the rock next to her, hopping in excitement. *The Chanted Kingdom will have a new queen!* His voice entered Lexa's mind telepathically.

I'm just happy someone dethroned the Snow Queen, Lexa replied.

Isn't she your half-sister? Hackett asked, and Lexa was certain that if the seagull had brows, he would have lifted one. Nonetheless, he cocked his head to the side.

Lexa frowned at him in annoyance. With all the thoughts weighing heavy on her mind, the last thing she needed was to be reminded of her wretched half-sister. Leave it to Hackett to always speak without thinking. She went back to mixing the poultice without dignifying his question with a response.

Hackett hopped on her leg and looked up at her. *Have you spoken to your father?*

Why don't you tell me more about this new queen? Lexa asked, skirting around the question.

Oh, her name is Snow White! he said excitedly, not even noticing she had purposely changed the subject. *And she's getting married today! Did you know she can also communicate with animals?*

That I've heard.

Lexa didn't know Snow personally, but she knew that anyone would've made a better queen than Aria. Though, she was happy to hear that Snow was kinder than most humans. According to Bob, the up-tight lobster who also happened to be her father's most trusted advisor, Snow saved him recently from a boiling pot. He was saved from certain death and almost made into dinner. She somehow was able to communicate with him and handed him over to her pet owl, who then dropped him back into the ocean.

If Lexa had to hear his survival story one more time, she would permanently cover her ears with seashells. Bob already hated the surface and couldn't say enough about how dangerous the humans were. But what about Snow? Wasn't she nice to him? Surely, not all humans were bad. He was just paranoid because of her father's disapproval of the land and its people.

Lexa clenched her jaw. Thinking about her father stirred up an anger that she took great effort to suppress. All her life, he had forbidden her from going to the surface, from interacting with the humans, and yet, he had a child with a human after Lexa's mother died.

All those years, he made her feel like she was odd for being drawn to the land, when in reality, she was just like him. Though, unlike him, Lexa never got to experience the land to the full as he had.

Lexa enjoyed the heat of the sun on her face, the fresh air blowing through her hair, and the warm sand between her toes. Even though her father knew she would go to the surface from time to time, he had no idea she had the means to generate legs. Thanks to the stone she traded with Aria, Lexa was able to connect with a stone her mother had given her. The two stones fit together like yin-and-yang, and once joined, they gave Lexa the ability to shift into human form. Even if only for a short time. It was just enough for her to enjoy the island she found in the middle of the sea.

More fireworks of red, white, and green exploded like confetti in the distance, and birds' songs traveled melodically through the swaying trees.

The animals were euphoric with the new queen's wedding, the buzz of excitement flowed through the air, and all life in the Chanted Forest sang and danced with glee.

Lexa had never heard of a human who could communicate with animals, and it was rare for them to honor and praise a human. So, whoever Snow was, she had to be special.

Lexa.

The corners of her mouth twitched at the familiar sound of her best friend. His voice was unmistakable, light, charming, and that day, he was jovial. She turned to find Jinko, her dolphin, appearing on the surface of the water. He was tangled up in a long string of algae that wrapped around his head and nose—though this did nothing to dampen his happy mood. Lexa tilted her head as she studied him.

Oh, Jinko.

She placed the jar aside, then leaped into the water. *What happened?*

I was being very careful, he said as she untangled him. *But then your father found me and asked about you.*

Lexa gave Jinko a horrified look.

Don't worry, he said. *I had already left your cave. But when I told him I didn't know where you were, I don't think he believed me. We might need to come up with a good story to throw him off our track.*

Despite the seriousness of the situation, Jinko spoke like they were playing a game and he merely wanted to talk strategy.

Why should I hide from him? Lexa grunted, freeing Jinko from the algae. *He lied to me my whole life.*

Jinko wiggled, then swam around a few times. *He wanted me to tell you that he needed to talk to you. I think he might be ready to tell you the truth.*

He didn't even try to hide the excitement in his voice. Jinko was an optimist, always thinking the best of people, but his optimism was lost on Lexa, especially when it came to her father.

What truth? Lexa's brows furrowed. *That he moved on from my mother with a human woman? Or that I'm related to Aria, of all people?*

Jinko pushed his nose onto Lexa's cheek. *You did save her life once.*

I did it for Jack, Lexa clarified. *He saved my life, and I could tell he wasn't going to let me save him unless I saved her too.*

What about the handsome pirate? Jinko asked with googly eyes. *Why did you save his life?*

The pirate's name was Ryke, and Jinko knew why she had saved his life. He knew that all it took was one look at his dark hair and piercing blue eyes, and her heart was claimed. She could no longer see a life, or even an existence, without him in it. Even if he was a pirate.

Except, since he couldn't breathe underwater, that was never going to be part of her reality. Even if she did save his life after the shipwreck and spent weeks nursing him back to health, they could never have a future together. He couldn't live with her under the sea, and she couldn't have legs for more than a few hours in a day. So, the land was not a viable option, either. But even if they found a way to beat the odds and conquer the impossible, he was still a pirate. Her father would never allow such a union. Pirates were the most formidable enemies of mermaids.

A life with Ryke was nothing but a mere dream. One that was coming to an end, sooner rather than later.

Do I have a blowfish in my mouth? Jinko asked, snapping Lexa from her thoughts. *It hurts when I try to swallow.*

He opened his mouth to reveal a large piece of metal curved at an angle, piercing his tongue. *Oh, no. It's a shark fork!* Lexa carefully removed it with a light tug, then held it up.

Why is it called a shark fork? Jinko asked, flipping his head from side to side as though shaking off the sting on his tongue.

No idea. Lexa turned to the seagull who was still on the rock. *Do you know?*

Why, of course. Hackett hit his beak on the metal a few times, then cocked his head. *For humans, a fork pierces food. This large one…* He beaked the metal again, *pierces shark food.*

Jinko's eyes grew wide. *Whoa.* Evidently, he

was enthused at the idea of almost swallowing such a useful object.

Lexa examined the metal even more carefully. *Interesting.*

It's also a scratcher for whales, Hackett added. *Whales get very scratchy, you see. This nifty gadget does the perfect job at scratching those hard-to-reach areas.*

Lexa sat up on the large, smooth rock and reached for the jar again.

What is that? Jinko asked, nudging her iridescent fin.

It's for Ryke's injury, Lexa answered, holding up the jar, the almost-transparent paste glistening in the sun like diamonds. *He's almost fully healed.*

Her smile faded as a wave of sadness washed over her.

Does that mean he's leaving? Jinko asked, his voice laced with disappointment for the first time.

Lexa shrugged, her face downcast. *It was going to happen sooner or later. He couldn't just live on this island forever.*

Can you ask him to stay?

Lexa shook her head, but not before smiling briefly at Jinko's naivety. *If only it were that simple. I couldn't do that to him.*

Why not? Jinko asked. *You saved his life. You nursed*

him back to health.

It still wouldn't be fair to him, she said. *Not when all I have to offer is a couple of hours in a day.*

With true love, all things are possible, right? Jinko countered, resting his head sideways on her lap so he could look up at her.

She smiled and caressed his head. *Not this time, unfortunately.* She let out a long sigh. *Well, I better find him before my father sends Bob looking for me.*

Jinko sank back into the water, and she reached for her necklace with both mermaid stones hanging on it. She fit them together, and with immediate effect, her tail split in two and transformed into legs.

She let out a giddy laugh, riveted by the feeling of her toes wiggling. Jinko made a cheerful sound as he lifted out of the water and pushed himself backward using his tail like a happy dance.

Lexa stood and turned to Jinko. *I'll see you soon.*

She jumped from the rock to the warm sand with a giddy smile. The feeling of her weight on the ground, held up by two feet and wobbly legs, was unlike anything she'd ever experienced before she got her necklace. Even though she had walked several times, it was still fascinating. She supposed the novelty of having legs might never truly wear off.

She grabbed the bundle of human clothes, which she kept hidden by the rock, then reached for a satchel. She shoved the shark fork in the bag along with the jar of poultice. Throwing her bag over her shoulder, she headed into the island.

On her way toward the other side of the island, she foraged legumes and fruits and shoved them into her bag. From a distance, she spotted Ryke, shirtless and waist-deep in the water, holding a makeshift spear in his hand.

She stopped walking for a moment and watched longingly as drips of water slid down his chiseled back. His strong arm lifted the spear over his head, and that was when she realized what he was about to do.

Fishermen alert! Away from the shore, now!

The fish must've scattered, because Ryke lowered the spear, scratching his head. Lexa watched him look around with confusion, as if wondering what just happened.

She smiled, then continued on her way toward him. When he noticed her approaching, a beaming smile spread across his face. He held Lexa captive with his piercing eyes. Her heart thumped so hard it hurt, but she gritted her teeth and tried to ignore it.

"Hey!" He waved. "Where did you go? I was looking everywhere for you."

She held up her bag. "I went to find some food."

"I was trying to get us some protein, but…" He pointed to the water. "I haven't been able to catch any fish in all the weeks I've been here."

Lexa settled under his makeshift hut, then turned her bag upside down over a thick cloth. "Chickpeas are a wonderful source of protein."

He walked out of the water. Glistening droplets slid from broad shoulders to his narrow waist. He came to sit next to her, then looked at the pile of legumes and fruits. "What did you get?"

She handed him a papaya. "Have you ever had one of these? They're delicious!"

Ryke arched a brow, and Lexa wondered if that had been a silly question. Did all humans eat papaya? She had only recently discovered it, and Hackett told her it was a fruit only eaten by royal humans… and goats. According to Hackett, papaya was most loved by goats.

Ryke removed the knife from the tip of his

spear, then as he was about to cut the fruit, he stared at it for a moment, his brows knitted together.

"Something wrong?" Lexa asked.

He offered her a soft smile. "Such a small thing, but... I can't even hold a fruit."

Lexa lowered her eyes to his left hand. Or lack thereof. He'd lost it during the shipwreck. She'd tried her best to treat it. The stump looked a lot better than it did weeks prior—the wound itself was no longer seeping, and a red raw layer of skin had grown over it. She had a feeling the mental healing would take a lot longer than the physical.

She frowned. "I'm sorry."

He shook his head. "You have nothing to apologize for. If it hadn't been for you, I wouldn't even have survived." He turned to face her, and his blue eyes locked with hers. "And for that, I will be eternally grateful."

Her green eyes dropped to his wet lips, so shiny and smooth, and her stomach fluttered. She looked away and sucked in a nervous breath to steady herself. She had never been attracted to a human before, let alone a pirate. But whenever she was in Ryke's presence, he made her feel things she never knew existed.

"I made something for you," she said, digging into her satchel and pulling out the jar with her own version of a poultice. "It's made with mermaid healing oil. It should help with the scar tissue."

By the time she turned around, Ryke had already sliced the papaya down the middle and was about to grab a chunk with his hand.

"Wait, I have a fork!" She beamed, digging into her satchel again.

"You do?"

She pulled out the large, curved metal attached to a leather handle. "Here..." She handed it to him with a wide smile.

He stared at it, confused. "A hook?"

"It's a shark fork," she added. "But it pierces food just the same. I washed it in the ocean, so it's clean, but it might taste a little salty."

An amused smile spread across Ryke's lips. "Thank you."

She smiled. "You're welcome."

He used the curve of the metal to scrape off the seeds from inside of the papaya. After cutting it in small chunks, he used the tip of his knife to pierce the bits of chopped up fruit.

He fed her a few pieces, and the explosion of

sweetness made her eyes roll back. She let out a moan. When her eyes opened again, she caught the look of amusement on Ryke's face as he watched her.

He cleared his throat and devoured the rest as if he hadn't eaten in weeks. But of course he had. She had made sure he got enough nutrition. Though, he did look thinner than when she had first brought him there.

Guilt tugged at the pit of her stomach. By that point, she could have taken him to the marina and allowed him to go back home. Even though she'd spent months convincing herself that she wanted him to heal fully, and that mermaid's healing components were a lot stronger than herbs from the land, Lexa knew the real reason she hadn't helped him leave the island was because she wanted to spend more time with him.

That wasn't the case in the beginning, though. After the shipwreck, when she first found him floating in the water, surrounded by his own blood, she had to find the nearest piece of land. That was why she brought him to the island. She needed to stabilize him. Several of his ribs had been cracked, he had lost a lot of blood from having lost his hand, and she could tell by the bruises on his body that he had internal injuries. The damage was far too extensive for any human healers to handle.

"What are you thinking about?" Ryke asked as he finished eating.

In the distance, Lexa could see the small wooden boat they built together. It was ready, and she knew he would be leaving soon. She offered him a sad smile, then reached for the jar she had placed aside.

"May I?" she asked, removing the top and scooping the thick paste with four of her fingers.

He placed his forearm on her lap. In silence, she began rubbing the poultice over his scar. Despite the gentle ebb and flow of the waves on the shore, it did little to soothe the pain building up in her heart.

After rubbing the medicinal paste over his scar, she grabbed her cloak and ripped a large chunk of the fabric. She wrapped it around his stump.

"Wait…" Ryke reached for the hook she had given him and shoved it into the cloth. "Go ahead and wrap it around this. Make sure it's tight and secure."

Lexa did as he asked. Once she was done, he lifted it up and examined the hook.

"Not a bad idea," he said, turning to her with a smile. "Thank you."

She tried to smile back, but her heart was too heavy.

"Hey…" He leaned forward and touched her face, rubbing her cheek softly with his thumb. "Don't look at me like that."

"Like what?"

He frowned. "Like you're never going to see me again."

"But the boat's ready and…" She swallowed through the lump in her throat. "You can't stay here forever."

"Then come with me." Ryke's lips barely moved, but the words landed in her heart like a thunderstorm. "Just because you've never been away from this island doesn't mean you should stay here alone."

Another wave of guilt tugged at the pit of her stomach. She had lied to him. But how else was she going to explain being stranded on a deserted island?

His gentle touch on her cheek sent flutters down her spine. "Let me show you the beautiful world that's out there. I promise, you won't regret it."

There was nothing she wanted more than to see the world, especially with him by her side, but that couldn't be her reality. "I wish I could."

"What's holding you back?" he asked. "There's nothing here for you."

"You wouldn't understand."

"Then help me understand." His deep blue eyes were so intense, she had to look away for fear he might read her thoughts.

"I just can't. I'm sorry." She rose to her feet with her heart aching. "You should just take the boat and go. Go home to your family. To your… whoever else has been waiting for you."

Ryke stood with her. "I'm a pirate," he said, his voice soft and tempting. "There is no one waiting for me. I don't even have a home." He blocked her view of the ocean. His blue eyes glistened in the sun as he watched her. "I have always felt alone in this world… until I met you."

She cupped his face, his scruffy stubble prickling against her palms. Unable to fight against the gravitational pull between them any longer, she leaned in and pressed her lips to his.

A wave of warmth washed over her as his

arms wrapped around her waist. He pressed his body against hers, and she found his tongue. The sweet taste overtook her senses, and she moaned against his mouth. His strong arms tightened around her, and she wanted that moment to never end. Abandoning her worries and all of the reasons she had that they couldn't be together, Lexa kissed Ryke with every bit of passion she had bottled up for weeks. Suddenly, in his arms, she pushed away every thought screaming in her mind, telling her why she couldn't be with him.

A sudden loud and panicked warning call came from the water, and Lexa ripped herself from Ryke's lips. She turned to the ocean and spotted Jinko jumping out of the water and flipping in the air.

We have to go now! His voice entered her mind like a siren, a stark contrast to his usual upbeat attitude from before. *It's your father!*

Lexa ran to the shore with the hairs on the back of her neck standing on end, then stopped when her feet hit the water. *What happened?*

Jinko flipped side to side, making a succession of squeaks, and the sound he made resembled that of a cry of devastation. Lexa's heart squeezed in her chest.

Your father was taken!

Lexa stopped breathing, and her heart raced even faster. Ryke came to stand next to her and put a hand on her shoulder.

"Are you all right?" he asked.

She stepped away from him and walked farther into the water. Usually, she would wait until she was on the other side of the island, and certain that Ryke would not see, before she turned back into a mermaid. But her father was in trouble and there was no time.

"I'm sorry," she whispered, pulling her mermaid stone apart. Within seconds, her iridescent fin appeared, and she slipped into the water.

Ryke jerked back with his eyes wide. He stumbled to the ground and gripped the sand as if his mind was spinning. But his eyes never left her as she swam away.

With an aching heart, she gave Ryke one last glance, just in case that was the last time she ever saw him. He opened his mouth to say something, but she had to go.

Lexa turned away and dove into the water with only one other thought in her mind. One urgent thought that overtook all others.

Who could've possibly taken her father?

CHAPTER TWO

RYKE

*R*yke stared at the spot in the ocean where Lexa had been. His mind spun with memories of their weeks together. But one memory burned in his mind more than all others.

He'd seen that mermaid before.

In the galleon with Jack and Aria before the ship wrecked. The mermaid that was caught in the net by the sailors. Ryke hadn't taken a good look at her face, but the long, black hair and shimmering fin had definitely caught his attention.

How had he not noticed that the mermaid and the woman who had nursed him back to health were the same person?

All the times she'd disappeared for almost a whole day, and he couldn't find her anywhere on the island. He should've thought about that possibility, but… she had legs.

In all his time as a pirate, he'd grown to learn a lot about mermaids. How their singing was their weapon. How their scales had healing properties. But never had he heard that they could generate legs. Which was why the possibility of Lexa being a mermaid never crossed his mind.

But she was a mermaid. And she had taken care of him, knowing he was a pirate. Could that have been why she didn't tell him the truth about who she was? Did she think he wouldn't have accepted her? Or perhaps she thought he would have betrayed her?

Whatever the case, he needed to talk to her.

Ryke rushed toward the boat they had spent weeks building together. He pushed it into the water, then hopped inside, allowing the waves to take him deeper toward the open sea.

"Lexa!" he yelled, squinting at the vast ocean ahead. "Come back!"

He grabbed the paddles and began to row. The wood slid off his metal hook. He lunged to grab it, but it disappeared into the water. He punched the side of the boat with his hook, burying the tip into the wood.

"Lexa!" he yelled again, frustration evident in his tone. Why did she have to leave without even giving him a chance to tell her he didn't care that she was a mermaid?

He needed her to know that nothing had changed for him.

"Lexa, where are you?" he yelled, looking around the vast ocean. "Please, come back and talk to me!"

Something hard hit the boat, and Ryke grabbed onto the sides. A rubbery fin broke through the surface of the water, and Ryke's heart raced in his chest. For a moment, he thought it was a shark as it swam around the boat, but then the animal lifted its head above the water, and he realized it was a dolphin.

He made a sound similar to what Ryke had heard on the shore. The same sound that had caught Lexa's attention before she disappeared into the ocean. He must've called for her. *He knew her!*

"Hey, mate!" Ryke reached to pet the dolphin. His skin was wet and rubbery against Ryke's palm. "You called for her, didn't you? Can you bring her back?"

The dolphin lifted his head, and while still

making the same melodic sound, water spewed from his mouth, splashing Ryke on the face. He closed his mouth and pressed his eyes shut. By the time he opened his eyes again, a long string of algae had been wrapped around his boat. The dolphin bit against the algae before swimming away.

"Wait!" Ryke called out. "I need to speak with her. Please, bring her back."

The boat jerked into motion. Ryke grabbed onto the sides to keep himself steady as the boat began to follow the fin slicing through the water.

He smiled at the possibility that the dolphin understood his request and was taking him to where Lexa was.

It wasn't until Ryke started to see the sailor ships from a distance that he realized the dolphin hadn't taken him to Lexa. He'd taken him to the marina.

"No!" he yelled at the dolphin as the boat slowed. "This is not where I wanted to go."

The dolphin released the algae from his mouth and swam around the boat a few times, making the same noise as before.

"I don't understand what you're saying," he replied, assuming the dolphin was trying to communicate with him. "Just take me back to the island. I'll wait for her there. She'll be back. I know it."

The dolphin suddenly disappeared, and Ryke lunged to the edge of the boat, peering into the dark water. "Wait! Don't go! Take me back!"

When the dolphin didn't return, a tightness squeezed in Ryke's chest. The animal was gone, and he couldn't help but wonder if he had brought Ryke to safety under Lexa's orders.

No. She was not going to get rid of him without an explanation. If she really wanted him gone, she was going to have to say it while looking him in the eyes.

He knew, without a shadow of a doubt, that he would find her again. If it was the last thing he did.

CHAPTER THREE

LEXA

*L*exa's inky black hair whipped backward as she swam faster than she'd ever done before. Nothing could calm her racing heartbeat that banged like war drums in her ears. She kept telling herself that Jinko must have been mistaken.

Her father was not missing. He couldn't be.

Poseidon, King of the Sea and ruler of Atlantis, could not have been taken. He was too strong. Too powerful.

All the years of their disagreements and every sour word she had said to her father came spiraling back to Lexa's mind, sending her into a whirlwind of anxiety and guilt.

She shot through a school of small silverback

fish, not stopping when several of them cried out indignantly at being disturbed on their daily stroll through the reef.

Lexa didn't have time to warn any sea life to get out of the way. She moved her long slender fin with so much force—more force than she knew was even possible—that she shot through the water like a glittering firework under the sea.

Weak rays of sunlight looked like shooting stars as she raced forward. She swam deeper, and the light weakened, giving way to the light blue rays from her home.

Atlantis generated its own light. The city was made up of towers of rocks, glowing all colors; from seafoam blue to arylide yellow. Two strong mermen with giant silver blades stood guard at the steel gates to the city.

Upon seeing Lexa, their stern expression softened, and they lowered their weapons.

"Princess Lexa." One of them bowed, his long golden locks flowing in the water. But Lexa did not stop to speak to them as she swam into the city.

Swarms of fish scattered as Lexa approached, but not before she heard them talking in hushed tones.

I hear King Poseidon is dead. Fish food.

He's immortal, you plankton. I heard he's gone to the shore to be with humans.

One thing is certain; he is not coming back.

Lexa barely paid any attention to all the eyes beaming at her from the sea life all around her. The mermaids huddled in groups in the city grounds, and even the critters on the rocky surface watched her go. She could sense the tension in the city, now quiet, when the streets were usually filled with transcendental music, morning, noon, and night. The absence of the melodies quickened her heart rate even more, and she took a great gulp of water, as though the salty taste might soothe her.

To her great disappointment, though, it did nothing to calm her nerves.

Finally, she reached the palace and threw open the heavy doors. The hinges squealed, and she entered without a word. She couldn't talk. She couldn't even think straight.

Not until she saw for herself that he was gone.

Lexa swam into the throne room that was once teeming with fish and mermaids, but now vacant and eerily quiet. She looked up at the mighty throne made with a hundred tridents molded together. The silver glinted in the white orbs of light pouring down from the white rock ceiling. Lexa had pictured her father sitting on the throne with such intensity that, for a glimmer of a moment, she thought that she could see him, smiling broadly at her, spreading his huge arms and welcoming her home.

But then she blinked, and the vision vanished like a million pieces of glitter, and instead, a little red lobster sat on a step in front of the throne, its body trembling.

Long deep cries came out like a succession of rattles and Lexa's heart sank as she slowed to a stop at the lobster's side.

"Oh, Bob. Tell me it isn't true." She lowered to him and held out her hand for the lobster to scuttle onto her palm. He did so, turning his face to look up at her with the saddest eyes Lexa had ever seen on a lobster.

It's all my fault. I advised him to go.

Bob turned away, as though looking at Lexa was too much for his conscience to bear. *I'm so sorry. If I had known it was a trap, I would never have...*

"What happened, Bob?" Lexa asked, urging him out of his state of misery to fill her in on the situation. She needed details.

Someone told him you were in trouble with the humans and needed King Poseidon's help. He didn't even hesitate. He left, alone. I should have gathered more information.

The lobster hiccupped and snapped his pincers, muttering to himself under his breath in a moment of irritation.

I tried to go with him. But no creature in the sea can match the speed of the merpeople. By the time I reached him, he… he…

"What? Tell me, Bob. Tell me, what did you see?"

Though she was weightless in the water and bobbed up and down with her long hair snaking back and forth, her heart weighed heavy, threatening to drag her down to an abyss.

It… it was terrible. He was in a giant net, unconscious, and it was hanging from a pirate ship.

Lexa's ears rang, and every part of her body grew ice cold like she had taken a swim in the Arctic. Mermaids had few enemies, for they kept to themselves, mostly, and respected all creatures under the sea. But there was one enemy that all merpeople had grown to loathe. Pirates.

The pirates invaded the waters, dumping iron chains, stealing and killing schools of fish. But the worst crime they committed was that they hunted merpeople.

Pirates were mere mortal men. Land people. They were made of just flesh and bone, and did not possess the strength of someone like Poseidon, who could rip an entire ship apart with his bare hands, or command a vortex with a flick of the wrist.

The thought that the feeble humans were able to capture the King of the Sea was unfathomable.

But such matters couldn't be dwelt upon. Lexa forced herself to focus and turned back to Bob, who was sobbing on her arm. "Take me to the ship."

Bob looked up, frightened. *Princess, I mustn't. What if something happens to you, too?*

It's an order from your Princess, she said firmly.

Bob let out a sigh, then charged through the water, leading Lexa out of the palace and away from Atlantis. Once outside the city walls, he swam upward and took great gasps of breath, leaving a trail of bubbles behind him as he charged ahead.

Lexa was not out of breath, though her mind grew dizzy as she followed Bob in silence. The sea became cool and abandoned, and before long, they approached the surface. Bob stopped and gasped, then circled the spot, inspecting three large rectangular shapes floating above them.

It was right here. Look. The net!

Lexa swam up, and her face broke the surface. Misty clouds surrounded the murky waters, and rolling fog shielded the shoreline from view. The surrounding waters were empty. The hairs on the back of Lexa's neck stood on end as she cast her eyes around the scattered pieces of driftwood and a mass of tangled ropes floating on the water.

Bob popped his head out. *I found the ship! It's down there.*

He disappeared again and Lexa followed Bob downward. Finally, a giant ship came into view. Tiny specs of dust floated in the water around the sunken vessel, and Lexa knew the shipwreck must have been recent.

She searched the fallen ship for any clue that might tell her where her father had been taken, but there was nothing. She suddenly found herself wondering how many ships it must've taken to capture her father. Certainly, he wouldn't have gone down without a fight.

I need to find out where they've taken him. She whipped around to look at Bob, who had his pincers hanging limply at his sides. His eyes were still sad and forlorn.

How are you going to do that? There's nothing here.

Lexa looked up at the surface far above their heads, a scattering of daylight lit up the water, but she couldn't feel the warmth of the sun on her face. In the absence of the sun, and with no clue as to where her father was, Lexa grew colder.

I need to speak to a pirate. I need to go back and find Ryke. She balled her fists and clamped her jaw, determined. She wasn't sure if Ryke would even want to talk to her now that he knew who she was. Or *what* she was. But she had no choice.

Lexa!

A bleating of clicks and high pitch squeals drew Lexa's attention to look behind her. Jinko soared through the water, zooming toward her with a sense of urgency.

What is it now, Jinko? Lexa asked, uneasy by Jinko's nervous cries.

Ryke is gone. He got on the boat and started to leave, so I helped him to the marina.

The marina? Lexa clutched her arms, breathing in the saltwater and swallowing hard. If Ryke was on the mainland, he could be anywhere by now.

She touched her stone necklace and chewed her lip.

I can only have legs for a few hours. I'll never find him in time. And if anyone at the marina found her as a mermaid, they'd kill her.

Neither Bob nor Jinko replied as they swam around Lexa, both looking lost and in disbelief over the absence of their king. She knew they were silently thinking that all hope was lost. The trail had grown cold, and all that was left to do was give up.

But Lexa refused to give up. Not yet.

She needed to talk to someone who knew about pirates, and there was only one person left that she knew who could help her.

Too bad it happened to be someone who was hated by all merpeople.

But Lexa was out of options.

It was time to visit Neri.

CHAPTER FOUR

RYKE

Thick fog rolled in from the sea, covering the marina. But despite the haze, it was still bustling with life. Ryke could hear random chatter over the squawking of seagulls flying overhead and the low rumble of wooden wheels over the cobbled streets. But despite being back around people again, Ryke was less than pleased.

He gritted his teeth as the small boat floated to an empty dock. He thought about tying the boat to the post, but decided against it. It wasn't like he was going to need it, anyway. There was no way he would be able to return to the island on such a small boat and one paddle. He was going to need a ship and a crew.

"Oi, Ryke, you thieving scumbag," a grueling voice came from the end of the pier.

Ryke stopped. He didn't have to look behind him to know who had called his name. The guttural growl in the man's voice gave it away, and the heavy footsteps on the dock told him the man wasn't alone.

"Lads…" Ryke whipped around and flashed them his most charming smile, as he had done so many times in the past. The group of pirates furrowed their brows as they surrounded Ryke, balling their fists. "What a pleasant surprise—"

One of the men lunged forward and punched Ryke in the face. He fell to the floor with an iron taste of blood filling his mouth. He spit the red liquid onto the wooden deck but didn't move.

"Where is it?" the man asked, towering over Ryke. "And don't make me ask again."

Ryke rolled over on the dock and looked up at the man. It was the last person he wanted to see. One-eyed Joe. A pirate with a boiling temper, sharp tongue, and even sharper sword that he took great pleasure in sinking into the flesh of his victims. Such victims were the men who owed him money.

"I was actually on my way to find you."

"Is that right?" The man pinned Ryke's knee with his thick leather boot, making Ryke grimace in pain. "Then I assume you have an explanation as to why my galleon is gone?"

Ryke clenched his jaw, knowing the man's galleon was now at the bottom of the ocean. "I needed her for something urgent, but I promise, I will get you an even better one. A bigger one."

The man removed his boot, sending relief up Ryke's leg. But then he crouched and looked Ryke in the face, his breath coming out in clouds of tobacco and rum, stinging the back of Ryke's throat with every inhale.

"You have until the full moon. If I don't have a galleon on this dock…" He glanced at Ryke's hook, a grim smile spreading across his face. "I will rip off your other hand and feed it to the sharks. Do I make myself clear?"

Ryke nodded. "Crystal."

There was a pause as the man eyed Ryke closely. Ryke could almost see the cogs turning in the man's brain, as if he were deliberating whether to just end Ryke on the spot.

But instead, One-eyed Joe smiled and rose to his feet. "Let's go, fellas."

The group of men walked away, laughing

among themselves, but even after they had left, the smell of hard liquor lingered on the dock. Ryke wiped his bloody lip with the back of his hand, then stood, squaring his shoulders.

He needed to find a ship quickly, but not to pay off his debt. He wasn't afraid of the loan sharks. The more pressing need was finding Lexa.

A small boat would take far too long. If she came back to the island to search for him, he didn't want her to think he had left her behind. Perhaps thinking that he got spooked by the fact she was a mermaid.

But that couldn't have been further from the truth. Not after all she had done for him, all the nights they sat under the stars. All the time Lexa tended to his injuries, when she softened his heart with her gentle voice and eased his troubles with a simple touch.

He couldn't bear to have her think she meant nothing to him.

Resolved more than ever, Ryke marched down the dock toward the bustling crowd of fishmongers and sailors.

He was going to find her. If it was the last thing he did.

CHAPTER FIVE

LEXA

*I*f there was one place that mermaids hated more than land… it was Neri's cave. Lexa knew that just going there was taking a big risk. She had heard the rumors. Neri had once lived in Atlantis but was banished. For what reason? There were many. Neri was a rare species of mermaid; instead of a long glittering fin, she sported eight giant tentacles. And while all the other mermaids were known for their enchanting beauty with shimmering skin and slender physiques, Neri was big and strong, with exaggerated features and had the hottest temper in all the sea.

She was downright terrifying, and arguably a powerful ally when she lived among them.

Now, she dwelt in a solitary cave surrounded by raging waters and rocks so sharp, they'd cut a human's skin clean off on impact.

That was just how Neri liked it. She had never been one for company, nor for having friends. But she was ambitious and had made deals with many humans. Especially pirates.

Lexa was certain that Neri was not going to be happy to see her, especially since it was Poseidon who banished her, but she had no other choice. Neri was the only sea creature who most likely had the answers Lexa was looking for. And she was also the only one who could never resist a deal.

As Lexa neared the cave, water thrashed about, forming cyclones and algae spinning under the surface. Lexa carefully avoided them as she swam deeper, where no human could possibly go.

Neri's cave was an ancient site that once belonged to a human man who professed himself to be a god. The mouth of the cave was said to be the entrance to the Underworld, home of Hades. But Lexa knew this was merely a story to keep curious mermaids away.

The man had set up traps and hidden

passages that would only open if the adventurer could solve his ominous riddles.

But Lexa didn't need to go in the human way. Underneath the cave was a tunnel that led right to the heart, with the purest water in the world.

After the man died, the cave and its special waters became the possession of Neri. Rumor had it that the man made a deal with her and disappeared soon after.

Lexa bit her lip as she pushed through a mass of tangled seaweed blocking the underwater entrance. She hoped that, for once, Neri might not be in a begrudging mood.

The passage opened out to a vast craggy cavern. The sparkling ceiling of the cave was just visible above the surface of the water, but before she could swim upward, a voice jolted her to a halt.

"Who dares interrupt my slumber?"

Lexa spun around and spotted Neri on a huge ledge near the water's surface. Three of her long tentacles writhed like snakes along the cave walls, as though she was bracing to capture Lexa in one swoop and squeeze the life out of her.

"It's me, Lexa, daughter of Poseidon," she shouted, straightening her spine. Though she didn't want to die, she was not going to show Neri a shred of fear.

Neri hissed, and another tentacle draped over the ledge, snaking down the wall. "How dare you show your face here?"

Neri slid over the ledge and climbed down to hover near her, all eight tentacles moved like spider legs as she drew closer. Lexa stiffened, uncomfortable at the close proximity, but resisted the urge to move away.

The corners of Neri's bulging lips curved upward as though she could read Lexa's thoughts and found the situation amusing. "You need my help." The words came out like a delighted purr. "The Princess of Atlantis needs my help. What a surprising turn of events."

Lexa set her jaw, pushing her pride aside and thinking about her father. She pictured him hanging in a net like the one she had been trapped in on the pirate ship. She could only imagine what terrible things the pirates planned to do to him. Just because he was immortal didn't mean he couldn't be tortured.

"Trust me, I wouldn't be here if I had any other option," she confessed. Neri howled with laughter as though Lexa had just delivered the perfect punchline to a joke.

"And what, pray tell, makes you think I'm interested in helping you?"

"Despite our differences, we have one common enemy," Lexa said, trying to keep her voice steady. "Pirates."

Neri's face fell, and her brows furrowed as she stole a glance at one of her tentacles. The scars, Lexa knew, had been the barbaric work of pirates many years ago. "I'm not interested."

"My father banished you when he could have taken your life," Lexa reminded her. "He was merciful towards you."

"Merciful?" Neri's eyes flashed with anger, and in a snap, she struck a tentacle at Lexa like a whip. It coiled around her body and lifted her up to her eye level. Neri leaned forward, and her huge eyes bored into Lexa's, a low, guttural growl rumbling from the bottom of her throat. "Because of him, I was forced to live in isolation. And what happened wasn't even my fault. Your mother was the one who came to me."

Lexa's eyes prickled. Neri's words cut her more deeply than she could ever achieve with physical force. "I didn't come to talk about my mother," she said, trying to keep her voice from breaking. "I came because of my father. He's been taken."

Neri's face softened, and she looked at Lexa with a hint of surprise. "You mean to tell me the mighty Poseidon has been captured by *pirates* in his own kingdom?"

The hint of derision in her tone didn't merit a response.

Neri lowered Lexa but didn't loosen her grip. "My, oh my. I honestly thought I'd never live to see the day…"

"Is your hatred for my father so strong that you would side with pirates?" Lexa asked as if the word "pirates" was venomous on her tongue.

Neri scowled. "I would never side with those barbarians. But I am also under no obligation to help your precious family. Now, go…" She shoved Lexa, releasing the grip around her. "And don't ever come back."

"I know they captured you, too, many years ago," Lexa said, glancing at Neri's tentacles. "Those scars. They tortured you, didn't they?"

Neri hid her tentacles underwater with a hint of shame. "I see you've been busying yourself with tales of the sea."

"If you help me save my father, I will plead on your behalf. You'll be allowed to return to Atlantis," Lexa promised.

Neri cocked her head. "And who says I want to return?"

"Then I'll plead for anything you desire."

Neri narrowed her eyes, then traced her long fingernail over her lips. "How exactly do you think I may be of help?"

"Tell me where they took you and how you broke free. That is all," Lexa said. "Once he returns, I will give you whatever you wish."

The corner of Neri's lips lifted in a cunning smile. "Sounds to me like you're trying to make a deal, my dear."

Lexa gulped. "What if… I am?"

Neri tossed her long mane of hair back like a horse. "Then you should've led with that." At the snap of her fingers, a small white crab scuttled over the edge from the ledge above their heads, and hopped into the water, floating down and bringing a white scroll and quill to Neri. Her eyes glinted as she paused to grin at Lexa, then she took the quill and scribbled on the scroll so fast, the quill was nothing but a blur swinging from side to side. "There. Sign at the bottom, and I'll tell you anything you want to know."

Lexa looked away from the contract to give Neri a pointed look. "I will sign nothing until you tell me where I can find my father."

Neri sighed impatiently. "It was most likely a net made of threads of elven metal. It's the only element in this world that can weaken us, your father included."

So, that was how they were able to trap her father. "What about his trident?"

"Useless in the presence of elven material," Neri explained. "Why do you think your father chose to ally himself with the Elves? They are the most powerful beings in our world."

"Where would pirates have taken my father?" Lexa asked.

"I don't know where he would be," Neri confessed. "But I do know *how* you can find him."

Lexa leaned forward with eager eyes. "Tell me."

Neri fluffed her hair as if looking at her reflection in a mirror. "The King of the Shores."

Neri's words jolted Lexa back. "What about him?"

"It would be wise to address him on this

matter," she explained. "We may have eyes under the sea, but he has all eyes above it. If there's a ship in the ocean, he knows about it."

That made no sense to Lexa, and for a moment, she wondered if that was Neri's ill sense of humor. Perhaps she found some amusement in sending Lexa to an ambush. For she was certain that if she went to the King of the Shores, he'd have her captured. "We've been at war for decades. For all I know, he's the one who took my father."

Neri shook her head with a deep groan. "The King of the Shores... Oh, there is so much you do not know, little mermaid." She laughed derisively and dragged a huge hand over her face. "Taking your father would not be to his advantage because it would intensify the war. Besides, if there is anyone who hates pirates more than mermaids, it is the King of the Shores."

"How come?"

"Pirates have stolen many of his ships, and he would have them eradicated if he could."

Lexa frowned. She really didn't know much. Her father tried to explain the politics, but she never cared to listen.

"Pirates, on the other hand..." Neri continued. "Well, they sell mermaids to the highest bidder. And there's no telling what those men will do."

Lexa's arms trembled as a shiver took over her, and she found herself wondering if Neri had ever been sold. Was that how she broke free? At what cost?

"The King would surely be notified of an auction. Simply because he's known for capturing mermaids. No one knows he releases them. Especially for Poseidon. I daresay an auction like that will be… historic."

Lexa's heart thumped against her ribcage. "I have diamonds. I can outbid everyone."

Neri threw her head back and cackled, her throaty laugh scratched the cave walls and vibrated the water particles in the most jarring way. "Foolish child." Neri looked at Lexa again, her big eyes boring down at her. "Not only is it a private auction, by invitation only, but the moment you step on that island, they will capture you and make a royal package out of you and your father. That is why you need the King of the Shores to advocate for you. No one will question his motives, and not in a million years will they think he is helping you."

Lexa hated that Neri was right. But she did say something that caught Lexa's attention. "What island?"

Neri shook her head. "I don't know. I simply recall waking up in a tank, facing a room full of people watching me as if I was some sort of display."

"How did you break free?"

Neri's eyes roamed around the cave, then she turned with a wicked smile. "I made a deal with someone very powerful."

Lexa had heard rumors that Neri's cave had an entrance to the Underworld, and Lexa wondered if the powerful person who set her free might've been Hades. That would've explained a lot.

"How do I get the King of the Shores to help me?"

Neri pressed a finger to her painted lips. "Arrange for a meeting with him and find out his price."

"What if I can't convince him?"

Neri shrugged, picking at her nails. "Then Poseidon is as good as dead."

Lexa shook her head. That wasn't an option. "How do I get an audience with him? The King of the Shores is smart enough to avoid the sea. And I can only have legs for a short time." Lexa touched the two halves of her necklace and bit her lip.

"I can make it permanent, you know," Neri said in a silky tone, her gaze flickering to the two mermaid stones.

Lexa held her stare and swallowed. "What's your price?"

Neri backed off, her eyes wide and innocent as she flicked her hair back. "Tell me, what is your father worth to you?"

"Everything. Even my own life." Lexa balled her hands into fists, and Neri smiled, as though approving of Lexa's fierceness.

"Then this is going to be tiny. Hardly even worth mentioning, really." Neri held out the scroll to Lexa, who snatched it out of her hand and began to read.

"I don't understand…" Lexa said, looking up at Neri with suspicion. "You want to be in line for the throne?"

Neri swaggered forward, splashing water as she approached Lexa. "Should anything happen to you and your father… I want to be named Queen of Atlantis. In exchange for this minor political detail… I will grant you permanent legs."

Lexa frowned at the scroll in her hands, feeling the heat of Neri's stare on her. Time was ticking. Her father would soon be auctioned off and she needed to make sure the right buyer got to him. And she couldn't do that without legs.

Lexa, don't do it! Don't you dare!

Bob popped up beside her, heaving as though he had swum as fast as he could across the whole ocean, not stopping, to catch up with her.

What choice do I have? Lexa replied.

Bob's eyes drooped with sadness. *Do not forget what happened to your mother when she made a deal with Neri.*

His words stung at the mention of her mother, but the determination only grew at the thought of losing her father also. He was the only family she had left. Nothing could change Lexa's mind now.

My mother's deal went bad because she didn't follow through on her end of the bargain. I will.

Resolved, Lexa took the quill from Neri, who merely grinned at her like a shark watching a school of fish swimming on its way. When Lexa signed her name, Neri snatched the scroll back and snapped her fingers again.

The white crab returned, this time with a white cotton dress. The crab handed it over to Lexa, who gave Neri a confused look. But she wasn't going to ask what happened to the poor woman to whom the dress belonged.

She stuffed it over her head, and as the cotton soaked up with water, it grew heavy on her body. "A few things you should know," Neri said, her tone turning formal. She placed a fingertip on the two mermaid stones, and her touch alone glued the two stones together so perfectly it appeared as though they had never been apart. Lexa glanced down at the single pendant in awe.

"So long as these stones are joined, you will have legs. But as soon as they break, you will turn back into a mermaid. So, I highly suggest you protect it with your life."

Lexa's mind grew dizzy, and she frowned as she tried to focus on what Neri was saying. With a wave of the hand, the water around them shot up like a tsunami. Being underwater was usually a pleasant and normal experience to Lexa, but this time, a wave of panic shot through her, and the dress weighed her deeper and deeper.

"What is happening?" Lexa tried to say, but instead of words, a mass of bubbles escaped her mouth. She tried to move her fin, but she no longer had one. Instead, she kicked her new legs and thrashed about, trying to return to the surface.

Neri's eyes shone like jewels as she swam down, watching with great amusement.

Did I forget to mention? Neri's voice entered Lexa's mind telepathically. *So long as those stones are joined, you are human and cannot breathe underwater.*

Lexa sank deeper into darkness and blinked up at Neri, who gave her a soft wave, watching her sink. *Goodbye, Princess, do not concern yourself with Atlantis. I'll take good care of it.*

It was a trick! Bob yelled. *I told you not to do it!*

Bob's angry voice floated in Lexa's head, but her ears rang, and every part of her body shuddered. She forced her heavy limbs to take her out of the cave and as far from the treacherous waters as possible. Her body screamed out in pain, her lungs throbbing in a way she had never known before. She kicked and kicked and looked up at the weak sunlight pouring down from the surface. For a moment, she thought she saw the outline of a dolphin above her head. But then the sunlight faded, and the water closed in on her until she became consumed in darkness.

Is she dead?

    I don't think so. Let me check her pulse.

    Oh my goodness. Please don't tell me she's dead. I can't. Please, Bob!

    Be quiet, I can't hear anything with you clicking and squeaking at me!

Lexa coughed up a mouthful of salty water and took greedy gasps of air. Her mind spun with confusion as she tried to recall what had happened to her and why she was on land.

She sat up, the sunshine beating down on her so strongly that she was certain the water had begun to sizzle on her arms.

She grasped a handful of sand as she steadied her breathing and blinked through the sunlight to see Jinko's head poking out of the water. Then she remembered seeing a dolphin just before she lost consciousness in the sea. It was Jinko. He saved her and took her ashore.

Lexa's heart squeezed with gratitude. *Thank you.*

Jinko clicked and jumped into the air, falling into the sea with a splash again.

I'm so glad you're okay.

Bob scuttled to her side, praising the gods that she was alive.

Wait. If I'm fully human now… how can I still hear you both? Lexa asked. And she knew she was fully human because whenever Lexa used her mermaid stones to generate temporary legs before, she still had the ability to breathe underwater. Now, she almost drowned.

Maybe that is a gift that has nothing to do with whether you are a mermaid or not. Snow White also has that ability.

Lexa smiled at Bob's words. He could not forget Snow White. Perhaps he had a crush? Lexa chuckled as she stood and looked around, straightening out the damp dress over her body.

Jinko had taken her to the beach. The palace stood tall and proud in the distance with silver towers and yellow flags billowing in the breeze. Tall palm trees followed a neat line along the beach, and Lexa watched a little girl, with her golden hair in bunches, skipping out from the trees. She paused a few times to bend down and pick up shells from the sand. Lexa could tell by her fine silk dress that the little girl was from the palace.

The child stopped, and her head snapped in Lexa's direction. Lexa waved, unsure of what else to do.

"Are those shells?" the little girl asked, pointing to Lexa's chest. The wet dress shaped them in a way that was almost transparent.

"Yes, they are," Lexa said.

The girl cocked her head. "Why do you have them there?"

Lexa smiled. "Where I'm from, we don't have dresses."

"Lily!" The voice of a woman came from the sand dunes ahead. A young woman with curly blonde hair came into view. She was dressed in a modest dress that tied at the waist, and her hair was tied back to look like a pony's tail.

"I'm here, Mrs. Ella!" Lily's sing-song voice was so sweet and gentle, Lexa couldn't help but smile. "I was just talking to her about shells."

"That's nice, but you know we don't speak to strangers," Ella murmured as she approached, motioning for Lily to go and stand behind her.

"Forgive me." Lexa bowed her head. "I'm Lexa, Princess of the Sea."

Lily blinked up at Lexa from behind her maid with big curious eyes of blue. "You're a princess?"

"Daughter of Poseidon?" Ella asked. But before Lexa could respond, Ella bowed her head. "Oh, Princess. My apologies."

Lexa touched Ella's shoulders and waited for her to look up again. "I have matters to discuss with the King of the Shores. May I arrange to meet with him?"

"That's my uncle!" Lily beamed, rushing to take Lexa's hand and pulling her toward the castle in the distance. "I can take you to him."

Ella stepped aside, allowing Lily to lead the way. Lexa stole one last glance at Jinko, bobbing in the water, and at Bob, who was watching her from the shore.

Be careful, Princess. Bob's whisper entered her mind, and she gave him a nod.

I will.

Then she turned back to the girl and followed her into the trees.

CHAPTER SIX

LEXA

*L*ily took Lexa by the hand and hurried through the castle grounds so fast Lexa hardly had time to take a proper look at the palace before they reached a small wooden door.

"If you want to see my uncle, you need to wear the proper clothes," Lily said, opening the door with a squeal. Lexa frowned at her own white cotton dress, wondering what was wrong with it, when two small hands pushed the small of her back. She stumbled forward with a chuckle, shooting the small girl an amused look.

"Where are you taking me?" she asked, walking inside. But Lily shushed her, pressing a finger to her lips as she guided her up the stairs.

As they rounded the corner, Lily entered a bedroom.

"Wendy, this is Lexa, Princess of the Sea," Lily announced as she walked inside. A teenage girl with sun-kissed blonde hair was making the bed. She glanced at Lexa before looking at Lily with great intent.

"Go and get one of momma's finest gowns. She needs to look like royalty if Uncle is going to see her. Will you help her get ready? Will you?" Lily clasped her hands together as though to beg. Wendy looked at Ella as she walked in after them. When Ella nodded, Wendy curtseyed to Lily with a bob, then hurried out of the room.

Lexa took the opportunity to look around as Lily started singing, skipping across the room to a large wooden house standing beside a black iron grate and a hole in the wall. Lexa walked over and studied it with fascination.

"That's a fireplace," Lily said, standing next to Lexa. She beamed and rocked on her heels, apparently happy to be a tour guide. "This is my bedroom. Come and see my dollhouse." She proceeded to give Lexa a tour of every nook and cranny of the room, even introducing her to every single one of her rag dolls. All the while, Ella stood by the door.

Wendy returned, and Lily jumped off her bed. "Oh, I love the blue dress."

"Lily, let's give the Princess some privacy," Ella said, motioning toward the door. "Perhaps you would like to practice the piano for a bit."

Lily frowned but didn't argue. "Wendy will take you to the throne room to see my uncle."

"Thank you so much for your assistance," Lexa said, smiling at the young girl. Lily's cheeks prickled like two strawberries as she grinned back, then she raced out of the room and slammed the door shut.

Lexa turned back to Wendy and watched her give a shy smile as she held out the dress for Lexa to step into. "Thank you," Lexa said.

The blue gown was made of the finest silk, and a strange bone-like lining sat against her torso as she shrugged the poofy sleeves over her shoulders.

Lexa's mind reeled as Wendy walked behind her and began to lace up the back. She pulled tight, and Lexa grunted, but chose not to complain. When she finished, Wendy picked up a silver paddle with what looked like thousands of bristles.

"What is that?" Lexa asked. But Wendy didn't respond. She just kept working on the dress. Lexa watched the young woman for a moment.

"Wendy?"

Wendy continued as if she hadn't heard a thing. But then she looked up and caught Lexa watching her. The young woman's eyes widened as if she had missed something, and with reddened cheeks, she lowered her eyes.

Lexa touched her hand, then turned to face her.

I just wanted to say this dress is beautiful, Lexa signed with her hands. *Thank you for helping me with it.*

Wendy's face lit up, and she began to sign back. *How do you know how to sign?*

Lexa's heart ached as she thought about it.

My mother taught me.

Wendy led Lexa to a plush cushion chair in front of a mirror and worked through her long hair with the paddle of bristles. To her surprise, it combed it smooth, and Wendy looked at Lexa's reflection as she worked on her hair.

Tell me more.

Lexa took a breath. *Where I'm from, there is a powerful sea creature. She strikes deals, but if you don't hold up your end of the bargain, she… takes your voice.* Lexa dropped her hands for a moment and shut her eyes. Then she looked at Wendy again, who stared at her unblinking, as though completely transfixed. *It happened to my mother.*

Wendy blinked at her, but the depth of sadness in her eyes spoke volumes. Before Lexa could ask her any questions, the bedroom door opened, and Ella walked in.

"Excuse me, Princess Lexa." She curtseyed and held her hands in front of her. "The King is ready for you."

Lexa jumped to her feet so fast her shoe got caught on the bottom of the gown, but Wendy helped her find her balance.

"Thank you," Lexa said, breathless. She had no idea being human involved so much clothing. The blue gown spread out like a giant clam and would be completely impractical if she were in the water.

Ella held open the door. "If you will follow me," she said, keeping her voice gentle and polite. "He's in the throne room."

*L*exa kept her head held high, and the tight dress kept her back impossibly straight as Ella led her to a grand hall not dissimilar to the one in Atlantis.

Small water tanks stood on wooden tables with colorful fish swimming around, and shards of glass hung from the ceiling with oceanic blue reflections of light dancing around the marble floor. On a large throne of gold sat a tall man with broad shoulders and black wavy hair with flecks of gray under a crown. Lexa took in the sight of the many rings on his fingers and golden pins along his garment. He rose, and as his eyes landed on Lexa, he bowed his head.

"Princess Alexandria. Welcome." He took a step toward her, then reached out his hand. Lexa took it, holding her breath.

"It's Lexa," she said, watching as the King kissed the back of her hand. "Thank you for agreeing to speak with me." She was pleased that —despite her jitters and the shoes that pinched her toes—her voice was steady.

The King gestured to a chair, and Lexa took the invitation to sit. Having little experience with human furniture, especially furniture this lavish, Lexa struggled to perch on the edge. Her skirt fanned out so wide, it was like a giant bubble around her.

"Now, to what do I owe the pleasure of this visit?" the King asked, his bushy brows rising as his eyes glanced at her dress before he met her gaze.

Lexa gulped. She wouldn't be surprised if he were wondering if she was hiding a fin under the skirt. Mermaids were not known to be able to generate legs.

"My father has been taken by pirates," Lexa finally said, digging her fingernails into her palms and pushing through the lump in her throat. "I need your help to get him back."

The King stroked his beard pensively. "How could I be of assistance to you in this matter?"

Lexa tilted her head to give him a frank look. "I know about the mermaid auctions."

The King studied her for a moment. "I can see why you would think I participate in those events, but I assure you, Princess, I do not buy from pirates. Nor do I wish to harm mermaids."

"Do you know where the auctions are held?" she asked.

The King shook his head. "Though I have never been to one, I have heard that the location changes. That being said, I would not advise the Princess of the Sea to go anywhere near that place. Not unless, of course, you want to be added to their list."

Lexa straightened her posture. "That's why I need your help. Perhaps you can attend the auction for me, and whatever price they want, I'll pay. Of course, you will be rewarded as well. We have many precious stones in Atlantis that you wouldn't dream of finding on land—"

"I'll grant your request," the King said with a note of finality in his tone, "but I'm not interested in your stones."

Lexa didn't dare breathe, fearing what his request might be instead.

"I want a peace treaty."

Lexa's tense shoulders relaxed. "Oh." That wasn't as bad of a request as she had feared. In fact, it was quite reasonable considering how her father had ordered the mermaids to sink all of his boats across the seas. His request shouldn't have come as a surprise to her at all.

"Where do I sign?" she asked. But the King raised a finger.

"Not just any treaty, however," he added. "I need something more… permanent. Otherwise, who am I to believe you will hold your end of the bargain?" The King shot Lexa a look of suspicion, and she sucked in a breath, offended by his presumption.

"What could possibly be more permanent than signing a treaty?" she asked, narrowing her eyes.

The King locked his eyes on hers. "An alliance, sealed in the sacred bond of marriage."

Lexa swallowed back a gasp as the words landed on her like a tidal wave. "You want me to marry you?" she asked, panic rising within her.

The King sat back and chortled. "Good heavens, no. I want you to marry my son, the Prince." He rose and clasped his hands behind his back as he took a gentle stroll to a nearby painting. Lexa presumed it was of his son, because the man looked far too young to resemble the King.

"As you may know, my men need to cross the sea safely to deliver my shipments. But the mermaids present a certain challenge…" He went on, but Lexa was no longer listening. She was still reeling at his words. She hadn't imagined that the King would want a marriage alliance. The thought paralyzed her. But the King continued, unaware of the beads of sweat forming on her forehead.

"I'm losing too many men," he continued. "Too many ships. I simply cannot afford to fight the mermaids any longer. But at the same time, I cannot trust them. So, I will help you get your father back, but in return, you must agree to marry my son and forge an unbreakable alliance between our kingdoms."

Lexa kept quiet as the thought swirled in her mind. Could she really marry a strange human prince, even if it were in exchange for her father's safety? Could she truly forgo her own happiness for her kingdom?

The King turned to face her, his expression nonchalant as if he'd simply asked her for a piece of gold. "You are welcome to stay in the palace. My son shall be returning soon, and you'll be able to meet him and court him as you wish. Meanwhile, I will gather a crew to look for your father."

Lexa gulped but didn't break eye contact. She couldn't let him see the fear in her. With her father gone, she was Atlantis' leader. Their queen.

Her kingdom was counting on her, not only to bring peace, but most importantly, to bring Poseidon back. But they weren't the only ones who needed the King of the Sea to return to his throne. She also needed her father. And at that moment, she was all out of options.

"I accept your terms," she finally said. "I'll become betrothed to the Prince, but only if you return my father to me. Not a moment before that."

The King's face broke into a delighted grin, and as he began to walk away, Lexa jumped up, taking handfuls of her skirt and yanking it up to avoid tripping on it as she followed. "But how can you be so sure you'll find him?"

The King halted and turned to smile serenely at Lexa. "Because…" he said, placing his hands in the pockets of his dark pants. "For this job, we'll need a pirate. And I happen to know one who we can trust."

CHAPTER SEVEN

RYKE

The tavern was bustling with sailors. Normally, Ryke would be planning his next job and taking advantage of their drunken state to discreetly pry information out of them. Depending on their cargo, that information would get Ryke quite a few pieces of gold.

But he couldn't stop thinking of Lexa long enough to plan his next job. Their time together replaying on a loop in his mind was beyond distracting.

The rush of shivers he got whenever she touched his arm. The heat that rose to his face whenever her green eyes landed on him.

Life had been so much simpler when Lexa

was taking care of him, and he only wished he had never left that blasted island.

Despite his best efforts, he couldn't concentrate enough to even start a conversation. And he was pretty certain that if he even tried to speak, her name would slip from his tongue. Her taste still lingered on his lips. Their kiss had been so powerful. It was nothing like anything he'd ever known when kissing a woman. No woman had ever captivated him like she had. Her dazzling green eyes were almost hypnotic.

He downed his drink in one huge gulp, then slammed the glass on the wooden counter, hoping the sound would alert the barman to refill it without delay.

A man with a metallic breastplate approached and stood next to Ryke. Though he didn't say anything, he also didn't bother sitting down or asking for a drink. Ryke looked down at his own empty glass, pretending not to notice the puffs of hot breath smothering him from the guard who stood uncomfortably close. Ryke could've downed ten drinks, and he would still have recognized the gold and brown uniform. The man was a guard for the King of the Shores. And the King only sent out his guards when he needed someone brought to him.

When another guard came to stand at Ryke's other side, he had no doubt in his mind that they were there for him. If he didn't think of an escape quickly, he would end up dragged aboard their ship and across the ocean. And Ryke was in no mood to be taken.

He glanced discreetly over his shoulder. Two more guards stood by the front door with their hands on the hilt of their swords.

"The King of Shores wishes an audience with you," one of the guards said.

Ryke kept his eyes on the empty glass as if completely oblivious that the guard had been speaking to him.

"Ryke—"

"The name…" Ryke slammed his arm down with a thump, the curve of the metal glinting in the tavern lights. "…is Hook. Now, where is my drink?" He slurred his words to make the guards believe he was drunk. If nothing else, at least it would temporarily lower their defenses.

The two guards looked at each other. Perhaps the hook threw them off, making them reconsider if Ryke really was the man they were looking for.

"Why is this glass still empty?" Ryke yelled like an irrational drunk. The barman came and filled the glass, unfazed. Surely, Ryke wasn't the first, nor would he be the last, person to demand a refill.

Ryke grabbed his drink and stood. "Good day, gentlemen." Turning to one of the guards, he placed his hook on his shoulder.

The guard squirmed as the sharp steel dug into the mesh of his uniform.

"Oh, sorry, mate." He released the hook from the guard's uniform, then flashed him a drunken smile. "Cheers!"

He jerked the glass in the air, spilling the drink on a drunk burly man walking by. The man growled as he towered over Ryke and glared at him with menace.

"Oi, my apologies, mate." Ryke looked up at the man who was the size of a full-grown bear. And when he raised his balled fist, it was the size of Ryke's head. "Never mind. You probably hit like a lass, anyway."

The man roared like an ogre, then swung his fist. Ryke ducked, causing the blow to hit the guard behind him. When the guard fell to the floor, Ryke pushed the other guard into a group of drunken sailors to his left. Their drinks spilled over the table, and they jumped to their feet with their brows furrowed.

Before long, the entire tavern broke into a fight. The guards by the door tried pushing their way through, but the chaos slowed them down. Ryke jumped over the counter and ran toward the back door. He couldn't stop himself from laughing as he weaved through the narrow halls toward the exit.

But as soon as he stepped outside, he was forced to a halt. Six guards stood in the alley with their swords drawn, blocking his path.

"You are coming with us," one of the guards said firmly.

Ryke flashed them a challenging smile, then drew his sword. "Not without a fight."

*R*yke opened his eyes and blinked up at the arches of gold in the ceiling. Paintings of cherubs and mermaids were looking down on him, and he inhaled deeply as his sleepy brain started to put the pieces together. He sat up and squinted into the golden rays of sunshine beaming through the eggshell white drapes and sighed. He was at the castle. He pushed the silk sheets off his legs and climbed out of bed, arching his back as he stood. In catching a glimpse of himself in a mirror across the room, he noticed he'd been stripped down to his undergarments.

Did they really think that taking his clothes would stop him from running away? It never stopped him before. But then he saw his clothes lying neatly on a bergère chair in the corner. He grabbed his shirt, noticing how crisp it was, and smelled it. All traces of his sweat had been erased by the scent of fresh lavender soap.

How long had he been unconscious? Long enough for someone to wash, dry, and hand press his clothes, he supposed.

He touched the back of his head, and pain shot through his skull.

Cowardly guards. Real men stand face-to-face with their opponents. Not strike them from behind.

A knock came from the door, and Ryke hurried to get dressed. Once he shrugged on his long leather coat, he pulled the door open. No one was there.

He stepped outside and looked around. The

hallway was empty except for suits of armor lining the stone walls. He closed the door behind him and followed the red carpet down the corridor until he found the grand staircase. As he descended to the main entrance hall, his heavy boots echoed against the marble floor.

"Mr. Ryke," a voice came from his right. Ryke turned and spotted a butler with steel gray hair standing in front of a wooden double door. "If you wish to eat something, I can have it sent to you."

Ryke gave the butler a serious look. "All I want is to know why I was dragged here."

"Perhaps because you refused to come when summoned," the butler replied as if it was the most obvious answer.

Ryke narrowed his eyes, then went to stand in front of the old man. "Making jokes, are we?"

The butler suppressed a smile. "You make it so easy, sir."

"Why am I here, Arnold?" Ryke asked again, but in a much softer tone. He was done with these games. This time, he wasn't addressing him as the butler, but as the man who had once been his father's right hand. "I know you know."

The butler's stern expression softened, and he

looked at Ryke as if remembering the young lad who once lived in that castle. "The King is looking to make a peace treaty with Poseidon."

"The King of the Sea?" Ryke laughed. "And how on Earth will he manage to do that?"

"With your help. That is why you were brought here."

Ryke shook his head. "I don't understand."

"He needs an experienced pirate who knows more of the seas beyond the boundaries."

"What for?"

"To rescue Poseidon from the clutches of a group of pirates."

Ryke's amused expression vanished. "Wait. The King of the Sea has been captured by pirates?"

"Yes. And the Princess has come seeking the help of the King of the Shores."

Ryke's eyes widened. "Their princess came here?"

"Indeed. And I believe she agreed to the treaty, so long as her father is brought back safely."

"Where is the King?"

"He's in a meeting at the moment—"

Before the butler even finished talking, Ryke

walked around him and pushed through the double doors, opening them with a loud bang.

The King looked up from the end of a long rectangular table with many of his royal officials seated around him.

As Ryke stepped into the room, all eyes followed him. The two guards who stood behind the King touched the hilt of their swords, just waiting for the order to spring into action.

The King looked alarmed at first, but as soon as his brain registered that it was Ryke, he leaned back and smiled. "You're awake. Took you long enough."

Ryke bowed his head. "Hello, Uncle."

The King stood in his royal attire and made a dismissive gesture toward his officials. The room was silent for a moment. The group of men looked at each other with confusion in their eyes. It seemed that no decision had been made regarding whatever topic they had been discussing.

After a few seconds, when no one seemed to move, the King gave them all a pointed look. "Must I have to say it?"

"No, My Lord," one of the men replied, rising to his feet and gathering a stack of parchments from the table. The rest of the officials followed in, gathering their things and heading out the door.

The King shifted his attention back to his nephew and smiled. "Come…" He waved at Ryke to follow as he headed toward the courtyard outside. "Take a walk with me."

As they stepped outside, Ryke marveled at the glittering ocean, soft peaks of golden sunshine beamed from the sky, and the view lit Ryke's memory of the island. And of the mermaid who had saved him. He placed a hand over the cuff of his metal hook with a grunt and pushed the thought aside.

Though they were on the ground floor, the castle was still elevated above the beach, and there was nothing but sea and skies as far as the eyes could see. It was as though his uncle lived on the edge of the world. He took in the clear blue skies as a cool breeze washed over him. Seagulls chirped in the distance, just above the sound of crashing waves.

"It is a pleasure having you back," his uncle said as they walked side by side.

"This place looks exactly the same," Ryke replied. "And I don't mean that in a good way."

There were too many memories of his parents. His father teaching him to fight with a sword just off the shore. His mother drinking tea under the palm tree near the rocks. The ghosts of his past haunted him on those seemingly beautiful shores, and being back hurt too much. He couldn't wait to leave all of that behind yet again.

"Ryke—"

"It's Hook now." He turned away from his uncle and gazed out to the ocean.

"Changing your name isn't going to change your past," his uncle said in a soft tone. "Or your future."

Ryke clenched his jaw. "My future is out there. As far away from this place as possible."

"She misses you."

Ryke's chest tightened as if his uncle had reached in and grabbed his heart with his bare hands. "She's better off here with you. She's safe here."

"I agree," the King said, turning toward the beach. "But so are you. You see, I don't mind that you want to go off on your own and follow a different path. All I ask is that you come around once in a while. Don't abandon her."

Ryke swung around, concerned. "Is that what she thinks I did? She thinks I abandoned her?"

"Your sister is almost ten. She's starting to ask about you. Why you don't come around. Why you don't visit with her. And although she's believed my excuses thus far, that won't always be the case, Son."

Ryke was not his son, but he knew the sentiment came from a good place. When his parents died, his uncle took him and his sister as his own. The Prince had grown to be more like his brother than his cousin. Ryke owed his uncle everything, but he couldn't live off the royal family for the rest of his life. His father had taught him to be his own person. To follow his own path. And he wasn't quite done trying.

"So, why am I here?" Ryke asked, turning to face his uncle once again. "Something about a peace treaty?"

The King chuckled as he shook his head. "Seems the walls have ears in this castle."

"And mouths," Ryke teased.

The King nodded. "It's true. We have been offered a peace treaty with the Princess of the Sea. But only if we manage her father's safe return."

Ryke rubbed the back of his neck. "Where was he taken?"

The King pressed his lips into a tight line. "That's what I need you to find out. All we know at the moment is that he was taken by pirates."

"So, what exactly do you need from me?" Ryke asked.

"Which group of pirates do you think would be bold enough to snatch Poseidon and get away with it? And where would they take him?"

Ryke paced back and forth, tapping a finger to his lips. "A capture like this would require a ship with elven metal," Ryke explained. "Not only around the ship, but especially on the strings of the net. No regular rope could ever have detained someone so powerful as Poseidon."

The King narrowed his eyes. "Do you know who has a ship like that?"

"The Barbarians," Ryke said. "They are the only group that has never failed a job. I have worked on a few with them. In fact, that's how I won my ship."

The King turned toward the ocean. "Where is your ship?"

"At the bottom of the ocean, but that is not the point." Ryke waved it off. "The point is... The

Barbarians always lure their prey farther west. Something about the storms in that region that only their ship can handle. That's how they win. Every time."

The King stared at his nephew with eyes unblinking. "Fascinating."

"What?"

"How intelligent you are. I'm thoroughly impressed."

Ryke smiled. "Thank you."

"Does that mean you accept?" the King asked. "Will you join us in bringing peace between our kingdoms?"

"Yes. I will lead your men to the captors of Poseidon," Ryke replied. But not for peace or the kingdoms. After all, that wasn't his responsibility. All he wanted was to find Lexa again. He wasn't entirely sure of the rules of the sea, but it seemed like a good place to start.

"What else is on your mind?"

Ryke looked at his uncle. "Can this Princess be trusted?"

Even though Ryke would trust Lexa with his life, he didn't feel that way about every mermaid in the sea. They were treacherous creatures, especially the sirens, with their cruel intentions and weaponized songs. As for the princess, he knew nothing of her other than that Poseidon kept her under lock and key—or whatever it was that mermaids used underwater.

"I don't trust mermaids either," the King replied. "That's why I have arranged a guarantee."

Ryke cocked his head. "What sort of guarantee?"

"A peace treaty that cannot be broken," the King explained, a sly smile tugging on the corner of his lips. "A marriage alliance."

Ryke's brows shot up. "Who's to be married?"

"Why, Tristan, of course."

Ryke wasn't entirely sure whether to feel happy or sad for his cousin. He had always been a hopeless romantic. A sincere believer in true love. Ryke, on the other hand, was always the cynical one. But after meeting Lexa, he'd come to realize his cousin had been right all along. *True love really was the strongest antidote for a broken heart.*

"How does Tristan feel about this arrangement?" Ryke asked.

"He is not yet aware of it," the King confessed, "but he will be coming home tonight from the Northern Realm. We are going to have a ball in his honor, and the Princess will be given the chance to meet him."

"Wait. The Princess is here in the castle?"

The King nodded. "I have invited her to stay for as long as her father is missing."

"I would like to speak with her," Ryke said, trying not to appear too eager. Surely, the Princess would know how he could find Lexa. Perhaps she could even summon her to the shore so Ryke could see her again. He needed to tell her that their circumstances—him being a pirate and her being a mermaid—were no obstacle for what they felt for one another. Oh, what he would do to hear the sweet sound of her voice just once more.

"I'm afraid your personal matter with the Princess will have to wait until tonight," the King said, putting a hand on Ryke's shoulder. "I want her to be comfortable and feel at home. And you're known to upset women more often than not."

His uncle wasn't wrong, but Ryke knew how to behave when he had to.

"Perhaps you will do the honor of standing by your cousin tonight?" the King requested. "I'm sure he will appreciate having you here, supporting this arrangement."

"And if he doesn't?" Ryke asked. "Want this arrangement, I mean."

"Then mermaids and sailors will continue to die at sea," the King replied. "It is time to end this war, and what better way than with *true love*, right?"

That would only be true if the Prince of the Shores and the Princess of the Sea fell madly in love. Though, the odds of that happening that very night were slim to none. But maybe that was just the cynical part of Ryke's brain overtaking his thoughts. If anyone had the power and faith to defeat the odds, it was his cousin—the ever-hopeless romantic prince.

"So, you will stay?" the King asked, his hand still resting on Ryke's shoulder.

"Yes, I'll stay," Ryke replied. "But since I am working for you, I will need advanced payment for my job."

His uncle laughed. "Name your price, and it is yours."

"I need a ship." He left out the part about that being a payment for One-eyed Joe.

The King took Ryke's hand in a firm handshake. "Consider it done."

"Ryke!" A little voice called out to him, and

Ryke smiled. He swung around with his arms ready to catch his sister in mid-air. She jumped and he caught her in his arms, careful to keep the hook away from her.

"I can't believe it. You're home!" Lily cheered. "I'm so happy I could burst!"

Ryke gave her a tight hug. "I will always come back for you, Lily. Always."

Lily giggled, then suddenly her brown eyes zeroed in on his hand. "What's that?"

Ryke lifted his hook with a shrug. "I got too tired of reaching for my weapon, so… I turned my hand into one."

Her face beamed. "How splendid!"

Ryke chuckled at her innocence, then put her down. She yanked on the collar of his jacket and lowered her voice to whisper in his ear. "We have a princess in the castle."

"Yes, we do." Ryke tapped the tip of her nose. "I'm looking at her now."

"Not me, silly." She slapped his arm. "I found her in the ocean and brought her to the castle. She's so beautiful."

Mermaids usually were as beautiful as they were dangerous. He made a mental note to ask his sister's maids to keep away from the mermaid. At least until Ryke was able to speak with her and assess the danger.

"Will you play with me? I've set up afternoon tea with Mr. Fluffy and Viscount Snuggles!" his sister begged, tugging on his long leather coat.

"All right, little missy." Ryke ran his hand through his sister's soft curls. "But only one cup, okay?"

His sister squealed, then hurried inside the castle. As Ryke watched her with her golden locks bouncing, he was left with only one thought in his mind.

If the mermaid was as beautiful as his sister had described, the Prince was in for a treat that night.

CHAPTER EIGHT

LEXA

*L*exa stood in the room she was to stay in while the King searched for her father. However long that might take. There was excited chatter in the halls of the castle as maids and servants rushed past her door, their arms laden with odd-looking human objects. If Lexa had not been standing on a plush stool surrounded by maids working on her gown, she would have snuck out to take a closer look.

The human world held her in wonderment as she looked around at all of the things so foreign to her. Ella, who seemed to have been the head maid, knelt down and studied Lexa's dress with deep concentration while holding a pin between her teeth.

The King had assigned Lexa a group of
handmaidens to take care of her every need
during her stay at the castle, and the first job was
to get her ready for the royal ball.

But not just any ball. Lexa's heart hammered
in her chest. The ball where she would meet the
Prince, to whom she was to be betrothed. So long
as the King held up his end of the bargain, but if
the King failed to save her father from whatever
wretched pirates had him, she would be free from
the obligation to marry. She would also have to
leave the human world forever and rule over
Atlantis... without her father.

A wave of sadness washed over her as she
thought about the last time she'd seen him. She
had just discovered that Aria was her half-sister,
which meant her father had relations with a human
woman. He'd gone to the land and lived among
humans. Yet, for so many years, he'd prohibited
Lexa from going to the surface and interacting with
humans. It was hypocritical, and she told him so.
That was the last time she saw her father. And
calling him a hypocrite were her last words to him.

Every glance in his direction sent a wave of
dread over her, so avoiding him seemed like a

pleasant idea at the time. But if regrets could kill, she would already have turned into seafoam.

Now, all of that seemed so petty and insignificant. She needed to make things right between them, whatever the cost. Even if it meant that she had to marry a human prince to free him from imprisonment.

But could she ever love a man who was not Ryke?

Not that *that* was important in the grand scheme of things, but it did make her heart ache. And if the King was successful at returning her father to his throne under the sea, Lexa would have to leave her life in the sea behind and live with the Prince in the palace. On land. How would she adjust?

But it was for the best. At least, for her kingdom. With the tensions between the sailors and mermaids gone, and their union really bringing peace, then the sailors would stop hunting the mermaids, and the mermaids would stop sinking their ships. The war would be over.

Either way she looked at it, though, none of the paths led her back to Ryke. If she had to rule Atlantis, she would surely never see him again, and if her father returned, she'd have to marry another man.

She wasn't sure which option gave her more heartache because neither gave her Ryke. Lexa had assumed that if she would marry a human, it would be the pirate with messy black hair and a brooding disposition; except for when his eyes would meet hers. Then the broodiness was gone and replaced with a sparkle.

Ella tugged on her skirt with so much force it almost made Lexa topple off the footstool. Startled, Lexa took a steadying breath and pushed her thoughts aside. There was no going back now, and without the King's help, there was no way she could save her father. And that was her priority.

Wendy looked up from the tiara she had been working on and gave Lexa a curious look as though she could read Lexa's expression. But she didn't remark on it and returned to the tiara, fastening the last pearl onto it with concentration.

Lexa was surrounded by maids who were making small adjustments to the olive-green gown. There were so many layers of material, it weighed her down. If she were to step into the sea, she would sink to the bottom of the ocean like a giant falling stone covered in moss.

The maids were quiet as they finished their work, adding lace to the bodice, while Ella finished sewing the hem. Another maid tied Lexa's long dark hair with white lilies sitting in the braid resting over her shoulder.

Once finished, everyone stood back to admire their work.

"Wendy, is the tiara ready?" Ella asked, looking at Wendy to allow her to read her lips.

Wendy jumped down from her chair and handed a dainty gold tiara to Ella, who then placed it tenderly on Lexa's head.

It was as though the room itself sighed as the maidens clasped their hands together, resting them to their cheeks and looking at Lexa like she was the most beautiful princess they had ever set eyes on.

Lexa smiled, thinking about her mermaidens back in Atlantis. They looked at Lexa the same way. Even though mermaids didn't wear big fancy gowns or tie their hair into elaborate braids. They fashioned seashells into dress coverings with water lilies, Anubias, and all manner of coral. And her dark hair flowed freely in the water at all times.

A part of her already missed the freeing sensation.

"You're ready," Ella announced with a light clap. "I'll go and tell the escort to come for you." She and the maids filed out of the room while Lexa thanked them all for their help.

Wendy remained, eyeing Lexa carefully. *You're nervous,* she signed.

I've never been to a human ball before. I don't know anything about this kingdom or what I'm expected to do, Lexa signed back.

Wendy's face lit up. *What would you like to know? The kingdom stretches along the western shores and the small islands toward the outer region.*

Lexa picked up her heavy skirts and stepped down from the footstool, watching Wendy talk about the Kingdom of the Shores with rapt attention.

Most of the men here are sailors and fishermen. The food here is delicious, and our lands are known to grow some of the rarest fruit. And I've been told the whimsical mermaid songs roll over the sea.

Wendy's cheeks reddened as though she became aware that she was chatting too much and holding Lexa up from going to the ball. But Lexa was in no hurry. In fact, she was glad for the distraction.

Tell me about the Prince. Is he kind? Lexa asked.

Wendy beamed at her, delighted by the invitation to keep going. *He is the kindest man I know. And very fair on the eyes too, if I might say, Princess. Hair so golden it's like the sunshine on a summer's day. And a heart so pure, that he is one of the few people in this palace to see me. I do believe you will be very happy when you meet him.*

Lexa's stomach unknotted slightly. Knowing that the Prince was, at the very least, not a shark calmed her nerves. Perhaps being married to a man like that wouldn't be so bad after all.

Wendy shuffled a little closer. *If I may ask… what are the balls like where you're from?*

Lexa smiled as the memories surfaced in her mind. *Enchanting,* she signed. Then her eyes glazed over as she recalled the last one that she had been to. It was in celebration of her coronation as Princess. All of Atlantis had gathered in the palace. *If you've been told our voices are beautiful when heard from the land, they are a hundred times more pleasing under the water. The singing never stops during a ball, and the crabs beat drums. No one is still. Not even for a moment. It's just hours and hours of music and dancing.*

Wendy looked up at Lexa, her eyes shining as she beamed with admiration. *It seems wonderful, I wish I could go to one!*

Lexa touched her mermaid stone necklace

and wondered if she would ever make it to another one herself. But then loud footsteps came from the hallway, and her heart jolted.

Any last piece of advice? She looked imploringly at Wendy who gave her a reassuring smile.

Human balls aren't much different than yours. There is food, music, and lots of dancing. You will be fine. If you forget what to do, just look around and go along with whatever others are doing.

A knock on the door interrupted their conversation, and Lexa took in a breath as a man entered the room. Judging from his formal attire, Lexa supposed he was a royal advisor.

"Good evening, Princess. My name is Benedito, and I will be your escort."

"Pleased to meet you," Lexa said politely.

"The pleasure is all mine. Now, the Prince is waiting to meet you. Shall we?" The man offered her his arm, and Lexa took it. He steered her out of the room, and the two of them walked down the hall.

The music that filled the halls was not like the music she was used to. Instead of stirring voices and rhythmic beats of drums, there was a different sound. It almost reminded her of Jinko when he was excited. And a little like the song-birds in the spring.

Wendy walked quietly beside Lexa, invisible to Benedito, but to Lexa, her presence was a great source of comfort. She hoped Wendy would stay close by.

When they reached a staircase leading to the ballroom, Lexa got her first glimpse of a human ball.

Lords and ladies dressed in far too much clothing than seemed natural swirled about the floor. Dresses of blues, greens, and reds swooshed. And the back of the gentlemen's jackets flapped like the flags of a ship as they danced with the women.

Along the edges of the room stood banquet tables laden with all manner of food and drink. And to the far corner sat a group of ladies and gentlemen playing strange instruments. They used their mouths to blow into pipes and their hands to drag bows over strings.

Caught up in the moment, Lexa touched her necklace again, as though to check it was still there and intact. Benedito leaned toward a royal guard who stood at the top of the stairs and muttered into his ear. The guard raised his hand, and the music promptly stopped.

The sudden silence prompted the dancing to cease, and Lexa scanned the sea of faces. She signed discreetly to Wendy, *Which one is the Prince?*

With the light blond hair in the center. He's next to his cousin.

Wendy discreetly motioned to two men standing in the center of the room. Neither one had a dancing partner. The one with black hair had his back to Lexa, and he seemed to be conversing with someone, while the other stood sideways, listening to the conversation. His hair was indeed the same shade as the sun on a summer's day.

"Princess Alexandria," the guard announced with a booming voice.

A wave of hushed whispers crossed the room, and the blond turned to look at Lexa. He flashed her a polite smile, but it didn't reach his eyes. Did he not think her to be pretty enough, or was he just as nervous as she was?

She picked up her skirts and descended the steps with as much care as possible. But then the dark-haired man next to the Prince turned and Lexa was blinded for a moment at the silver hook where his left hand should've been. Then their eyes locked.

Lexa's heart thumped wildly in her chest so that all she could hear was the beating in her ears.

Ryke's smile dropped as if he'd seen a ghost, but his eyes did not leave hers. Lexa stopped breathing, unable to place a foot in front of the other.

It's him.

Lexa's knees weakened, and she wobbled so much, the King must have noticed, because he climbed the stairs and reached for her.

Lexa turned and thanked Benedito as she let go of his arm. He bowed and stepped aside. The King guided her down the last few steps. Wendy followed, keeping her distance.

Lexa swallowed nervously and focused on her breathing as the King walked her through the crowd of guests until they reached the Prince. His smile widened, his teeth gleaming like pearls. Lexa could tell it was forced, and it made her slightly uncomfortable.

"Princess Alexandria. It is my honor to be your acquaintance," he said with a slight bow, then kissed her hand.

Lexa looked around for Ryke, but he was

gone. She forced a smile of her own to hide her disappointment, then took the Prince's arm. "Please, call me Lexa."

The Prince bowed his head. "As you wish." The two of them floated around the hall, the Prince greeting everyone like an old friend. Lexa kept quiet, uninterested in having a conversation with anyone, her mind set on finding Ryke and wondering where he disappeared to. Was he even real, or was he a figment of her imagination?

After what seemed like hours on her feet, all the guests were seated at the long tables and the floor cleared. Lexa took another sweeping look for any sign of Ryke. Her heart leaped at the glint of a fork, mistaking it for his hook. And every dark-haired man gave her pause, but none of them were him. The room darkened, and a hush fell on the people as stirring music began to fill the room.

A group of women danced in the middle of the hall, performing flips and waving ribbons in the air in streams of pink and yellow. As the guests watched the performance, entranced, with oohs and ahhs, Lexa glanced at the Prince sitting beside her. His expression was of awe as he watched the dancers. He held his cut crystal glass in the air, his drink untouched. Lexa wondered if he was so consumed by the performance that he forgot to drink it.

Lexa wanted to get Ryke out of her mind, and seeing that the Prince seemed nice enough, perhaps it wouldn't be so hard. Trying to strike up a conversation was the least she could do.

"So, Prince Tristan, do you like music?" she asked.

The Prince did not so much as glance in her direction. Thinking back on what Wendy had said about him, she gave him the benefit of the doubt rather than jumping to the conclusion that he was ignoring her.

"I love music," she added, dragging her index finger across the rim of her glass until it made a sound. "Singing is a pleasant pastime…"

When the Prince finally turned to her, though his smile was present, there was sadness in his eyes. He leaned into her ear. "You're missing the show."

And without another word, he shifted his attention back to the dancing women. Never had Lexa felt so invisible. Was that what her marriage would be like?

Lexa resisted the urge to get up and run away, and she forced herself to think of her father.

When the performance finished, the servers lifted the brass covers over their plates, and to Lexa's horror, she stared at a dead fish lying across a bed of leaves.

Despite not wanting to, she leaned closer to the Prince. "What is this?" she asked, the blood draining from her face.

The Prince looked up, his mouth already full of food. "Is something wrong?"

Lexa picked up a napkin and held it to her nose to stop the cooked fish smell from nauseating her. "Do you not know where I am from?" she asked, her voice muffled.

The Prince looked at her puzzled, then at her plate, then back at her again. "You don't like fish?" he asked, incredulous.

Lexa's stomach jolted, and she jumped to her feet. "Excuse me."

She dashed out of the hall and ran out into the fresh open air. Tall trees stood like gentle giants waving in the evening breeze, and Lexa took deep breaths to calm down as she walked farther into the garden.

Wendy had told Lexa the Prince met her with kindness and felt seen. But Lexa only saw indifference in the man's eyes. How could she agree to enter a marriage with someone who was merely doing his duty?

It was not that she expected the Prince to love her, but she thought at least the two could have become friends. No doubt, in marrying him, she would be left so empty. If only Jinko were there, or Bob, she wouldn't be so alone.

Furious and confused, Lexa looked up at the gleaming stars and silently called out to the gods to keep her father safe. She sucked in the cool sea breeze, steeling strength to keep her end of the deal.

Just then, a rustle of movement drew her eyes, and she looked further into the gardens. In the distance, Ryke was pacing back and forth just outside a garden maze. As though he sensed he was being watched, he turned to face her, and their eyes locked again.

A shocked gasp escaped her lips.

He *was* real.

CHAPTER NINE

RYKE

Ryke stared at Lexa with eyes unblinking as she stood frozen at the top of the steps. So much about her was different, yet so much was still the same. He'd never seen her in a gown before, but her face was just as beautiful and sun-kissed as he remembered. The way her long hair fell over her shoulders. How soft the dark strands had felt between his fingers.

He looked away and sucked in a breath, unaware that he'd stopped breathing. His heart was racing and his mind reeling. He couldn't believe she would become another man's bride. The pain that came with such a thought was simply unbearable.

He shook his head, willing the pain in his

heart to vanish. But the tightness in his chest was unlike anything he'd ever experienced.

"Ryke!" Lexa called out in a hushed tone. Her soft angelic voice carried in the wind, landing on his ears like a gentle kiss in the night.

He followed the sound because he simply did not have the strength to resist, and their eyes met once more. But as he took a step toward her, he spotted a guard walking in the distance. Lexa followed his gaze and noticed the guard as well.

She gave him a quizzical look. Ryke froze, knowing that being near her was a terrible idea, but couldn't help but steal another moment with her. He turned around and walked into the maze, away from prying eyes. Once he heard her footsteps behind him, he turned the corner and paced around the small space. His heart thumped in his chest as he heard her approach.

When her footsteps came to a halt behind him, he couldn't bring himself to turn around.

"Ryke…" she whispered. Her soft tone was like a gentle caress, and Ryke longed to take her in his arms. But instead, he clenched his jaw, willing himself to stay put.

"Please, say something," she breathed.

He clasped his hook behind his back and

turned around slowly. Even with only the light of the moon illuminating her face, her beauty was just as striking.

There was so much he wanted to say, but he didn't even know where to begin. It took all of his strength just to keep himself from reaching for her.

"Why didn't you tell me who you were?" he asked, his voice low but firm in the enclosed space. Her eyes shone like two moons, full of concern, and did he see a hint of regret?

She stepped toward him, her gown glistening in the moonlight as it brushed his pants. "I was afraid you wouldn't look at me the same way."

Ryke stiffened. "So you left without even giving me a chance?"

"The night of the shipwreck, with Jack and Aria," she whispered, "you looked straight at me aboard that ship, but yet... you didn't even see me. If you had, you would have remembered that the mermaid you helped save that night was me."

Ryke winced, her words as sharp as a dagger in his conscience. As much as he didn't want to admit it, she wasn't wrong. He had seen a mermaid tangled in the net, but he was so focused on helping Jack, then Aria got stabbed, and the ship began to sink. Everything had happened so fast.

Lexa took another step toward him, and every nerve on his body set fire as the heat of her body radiated inches from him. He longed to reach for her waist and pull her close, but her frown stopped him.

"I never meant to lie to you," she added. "I kept waiting for you to remember, but you hit your head and could recall very little of that night. Then after a while, it just felt like I let it go too long. I was afraid you would be upset, and I couldn't risk you pushing me away. Not when you needed me to tend to your injuries. You wouldn't have been able to survive on your own, and I couldn't let you die. It was the least I could do for you having saved me."

He narrowed his eyes, a sickly sensation swirling in his midriff. "So saving my life was just… returning a favor?"

She stared at him incredulously. "Is that what you think? That after everything that happened between us on that island, that I was merely *returning a favor?*"

He didn't believe that. Not for a second. But

maybe he should. It would've made losing her a lot more bearable.

"Ryke, the only reason I left was because my father went missing," she explained. "That was not a call I could ignore."

"I'm not upset that you left. I'm angry that you didn't give me a chance to——" He pressed his lips together, then turned away from her. Even though the words were at the tip of his tongue, he held them at bay. He knew that the moment he poured out his feelings, he would surely collapse to his knees and be at her mercy.

She touched his arm, and a jolt of electricity shot through the fabric of his jacket. It took every ounce of self-control not to reach for her hand.

"A chance to what?" she asked.

He balled his fist. "Nothing."

"Ryke..." Her voice was soft and gentle. "Please, look at me."

He thought of a million reasons why he shouldn't, but then she whispered his name a second time and he could no longer resist the gravitational pull toward her. He turned slowly.

"Talk to me," she begged.

"What for?" He held her gaze. "Nothing I say will change anything."

"You don't know that."

"You're engaged to be married."

"Not yet, I'm not."

"But you will be…" His voice softened as the pain grew deeper. "As soon as I return with your father."

She opened her mouth, but no words came out. He could see it in her eyes that she knew it was true. They both did. A heavy silence washed over them, and all they could hear were the waves crashing in the distance.

"I never wanted any of this," she whispered, her eyes filling with tears. "But I have to do whatever it takes to save my father. Even if it means agreeing to a loveless marriage."

"The Prince is a good man," Ryke said, pushing through the lump in his throat. "Easy to love."

"Perhaps that would be true had my heart not been claimed by someone else."

Ryke's heart soared in his chest, but he dug his nails into his palm to keep it anchored in place.

"I thought leaving you was the hardest thing I would ever have to do, but…" Her piercing green eyes glistened in the moonlight. "Pretending not to love you will be the end of me."

A wave of desire rippled through him, awakening an unsatiated hunger that nagged at his insides ever since she left him on the island. He peered into her eyes. "And *you'll* be the end of me." With a growl, he pulled her into his arms and claimed her lips.

She gasped against his mouth, and he kissed her with as much urgency as a man dying of thirst and being handed a drink. She was the most decadent wine, invigorating his body as he tasted her. Longing to taste all of her. He deepened the kiss, and Lexa melted into his chest. She parted her lips with a moan that just about buckled his knees.

She grabbed two fists full of his hair and yanked on it until it was edging on painful. But Ryke didn't care, for in that stolen moment, she was all his, and he was going to savor every second he had with her. He lifted her by the gown until her feet left the ground. Her legs wrapped around his waist, and he pressed her against the maze's wall, pinning her with his body. The poker-hot heat of her inner thighs against his waist made all of his blood travel south. She moaned against his mouth once more, and he thought for sure his heart was going to burst into flames.

He tasted her tongue and nibbled on its velvety softness. He wanted her. Desperately. But she wasn't his for the taking.

And it took every ounce of his soul to rip his lips from hers.

"We can't," he panted, his body fighting against every syllable. "Not like this."

"I want you, Ryke," she whispered between ragged breaths, her voice dripped with desire and lust. "Even if just this once."

"I don't…" he said breathlessly.

She opened her eyes with alarm, only to be met with his serious expression. "Oh, I see."

He lowered her to the ground, and she smoothed down her dress with trembling hands. When he noticed she was avoiding his eyes, he lifted her chin.

"Lexa—"

"It's all right." She moved away from his touch. "My apologies. I completely misread the signals."

"You didn't misread anything." He drew closer and caressed her face. "What I meant was… I don't want you *just this once*. I want you, every night, for the rest of my life. For as long as I breathe, I want you to be in my arms."

"Oh." A beaming smile spread across her face. "Well, that does sound much better."

He chuckled as he combed her silky hair with his fingers until he reached the nape of her neck. "You're so beautiful." He leaned in for another kiss, but Lexa stiffened, giving him pause.

"I want nothing more than to spend the rest of my days with you, but..." She frowned. "It can never be anything more than a dream."

Ryke bit the inside of his cheek in thought. "Maybe not."

Her eyes widened in surprise. "What do you mean?"

"I will talk to my uncle," Ryke said, giving her a reassuring smile. "If it's a peace treaty that he seeks, there are other ways to attain it without you having to marry my cousin."

"Oh, Ryke!" Lexa threw her arms around his neck and pressed her lips to his for a long, savoring moment. When she pulled back, her mouth must've had some sort of gravitational pull because he leaned in and claimed them again. When her tongue found his and she moaned into his mouth, a wave of pleasure rippled through his body.

He pulled back, his desire warring against his instincts. "Soon enough," he said between breaths as he rested his forehead to hers. "I will be all yours, my love."

She sucked in a steadying breath, then nodded, her expression flushed. Ryke stepped back, giving her enough space to adjust her dress, trying and failing to smooth out the wrinkles.

"You should go first," he said, trying to steady his own breathing. "I'll wait a few minutes."

"Okay."

As she turned to walk away, he grabbed her hand and pulled her back into his arms. She laughed and kissed him until the very last possible second. Then she pulled away with a beaming smile and disappeared out of the maze.

Ryke let out a long shuddering breath, then leaned his back against the maze's wall with his heart racing in his chest.

He tried to do the right thing.

He tried to stay away.

But he simply couldn't… live without her.

*B*ack at the party, Ryke spotted his uncle across the room, talking to a lord and lady that he knew were from the north. A group of esteemed guests gathered around the King, and Ryke greeted them as he walked among them on his way to his uncle.

"My Lord…" Ryke bowed his head respectfully toward his uncle. "May I have a word in private?"

The King smiled, then tapped Ryke's shoulder lightly. "May business matters wait. Tonight, we shall celebrate."

The guests around him cheered, raising their glasses in agreement, and the King clasped his hands together. "How about another drink, gentlemen?"

The King walked away lighter than air while Ryke's heart weighed heavily in his chest. And it would only weigh heavier the longer Lexa was not in his arms.

Lexa.

He scanned around the ballroom until his eyes locked on her on the dance floor. She was waltzing with a burly man, and despite her best efforts, she kept stepping on his toes. The man didn't seem to mind, but her cheeks were beet red with embarrassment.

"My sincerest apologies, sir." Ryke read her lips as he made his way toward her. "Dancing isn't my strong suit."

Once in the center of the dance floor, Ryke stopped next to the gentleman. "May I cut in?"

"Certainly." The man stepped back and politely bowed his head. As he walked past Ryke, he whispered, "Good luck, I'm going to have to soak my ruddy feet in bath salts tonight."

Lexa's cheeks flushed, and Ryke chuckled.

"I'm assuming mermaids dance differently?" he asked, taking her hand in his, then touching the side of his hook against her lower back.

"Dancing under the sea is just as difficult," Lexa confessed. "A lot of swirling. If you're not careful, you can get dizzy."

Ryke laughed, and when the music started again, he looked her in the eyes. "Just listen to the melody," he said, guiding her gently. "Now, follow my lead."

"I would follow you anywhere." Her voice was like a soft purr tickling his senses and awakening a deep hunger he had been struggling to suppress.

He cleared his throat, then stole a quick glance around the room. "Behave. Or I won't be able to control myself."

"I prefer the latter," she teased, letting her body press up neatly against his. Her heat flooded through him as though he had been dropped in a warm bath.

He stepped back and twirled her gently. She followed his lead, and her dress spun elegantly around her. He pulled her back into his arms, and it amazed him just how perfectly she fit against him.

"So, do all mermaids have legs?" Ryke asked, hoping to steer the conversation away from his inappropriate thoughts. However, mentioning her legs was probably not going to divert it too far.

"Not every mermaid," she confessed. "In fact, not even me. The only reason I have them at the moment is because of this…" She touched the stone in her necklace. "Without it, I wouldn't be able to shift. And if it breaks… I lose my legs for good."

Ryke gulped. He didn't even want to think

about Lexa going back to the sea and never being able to be with her again.

"Does it break easily?" he asked, unable to hide the concern in his voice.

"Mermaid stones are robust," she explained. "But they're not indestructible, so… I should still be careful."

From the corner of his eye, Ryke caught his uncle walking out of the ballroom with a group of royal officials. He must've been headed for his study to smoke cigars.

Even though the King was clear he'd wanted to wait until the morning to discuss business matters, Ryke couldn't wait a minute longer. He needed to talk to him so that he could take Lexa with him. Tonight.

"My uncle seems to be in a pleasant mood," Ryke noted. "I'll go try to speak with him once more."

Lexa nodded. "I'll be here, wishing you the best of luck."

He stepped back, then bowed and kissed her hand. "Thank you for the lovely dance."

She curtseyed, then met his eyes with darkened desire. "The pleasure was all mine."

Ryke stepped away to avoid pulling her back

into his arms, then hurried after his uncle. He walked into his study just as he was reaching for the box of cigars.

"Uncle, I have a pressing matter to discuss with you that simply cannot wait."

"Oh. And what, pray tell, could be so pressing that it cannot wait?" the King asked, taking a cigar from the box, then passing the box around until each of the men took one. The smell of vanilla filled the air.

"The Princess no longer wishes to marry the Prince."

The King removed the cigar from his lips, and his expression turned sour. "Everyone out."

The group of men walked out of the study, leaving Ryke to deal with the angry man. "Guard!" the King called out, and a guard entered the study. "Bring me the Princess."

"Let the Princess be," Ryke cut in, bringing the guard to a halt. "I have already spoken to her. I am here on her behalf."

"On her behalf?" his uncle echoed. "Since when have you become an ambassador of the sea?"

Ryke waited for the guard to leave the room, then closed the door behind him. "Uncle, if it's a peace treaty that you seek, it does not have to be through a marriage alliance," he explained. "There are other ways."

"Other ways aren't guaranteed," the King replied with a scoff. He took a long drag of his cigar and blew out a puff of smoke.

Ryke paced the room, his nerves on edge. "But it can be. The Princess herself said that she would be willing to sign a treaty document that cannot be broken."

"A Princess doesn't have the authority to make such a treaty."

"But her father does," Ryke insisted. "And if we bring him back alive, she has given her word that her father will abide by her agreement."

The King stared at Ryke for a long moment, prompting Ryke to stop in his tracks and hold his discerning gaze. When he didn't back down, the King sighed.

"I don't trust them," the King confessed. "More of our sailors have died in those seas than soldiers in combat. I have a duty to protect my people."

"I understand that as king—"

"How could you possibly understand?" The King narrowed his eyes. "You rarely ever come around. And when you do, you want nothing to do with the family business."

"That doesn't mean you should force Tristan into a loveless marriage," Ryke said in frustration.

"Ah, now I see what this is truly about." The King nodded as he puffed the cigar. "Tristan put you up to this, did he not? Well, your concern for your cousin's happiness, however touching, is futile. Unlike you, he has a duty to this kingdom. And he will fulfill it. End of discussion."

"But why, if there are other ways?" Ryke pressed.

"Don't you think I have tried other ways to form this alliance?" the King asked. "I have been trying to attain a peace treaty for years. But Poseidon makes peace with no one. Except the Elves, that is."

"This time will be different."

"Yes, it will," the King agreed, bringing the cigar back to his lips. "Because this time, his daughter will be part of our family."

Ryke squared his shoulders. "I'm sorry, Uncle, but I will not lead this rescue mission under that agreement."

"As you wish," his uncle replied, waving his

cigar in the air. "As of this moment, you are relieved of your duty."

Ryke shook his head as if he'd just been slapped. "What?"

"I have plenty of experienced sailors that are more than capable of handling themselves out there. If you're only going to cause trouble, you're not welcome here. You can go back to whatever gin joint you came from. You're no longer needed."

Ryke stepped forward. "Uncle, please reconsider—"

"We are done here." The King's thunderous voice bounced off the bookshelves. "Now go. And close the door on your way out."

Ryke walked out of the study in a complete daze. Never had he imagined that by trying to help Lexa, he would have done more harm than good.

Now, the only way to save Lexa from that dreadful agreement was to find and rescue Poseidon before his uncle did.

CHAPTER TEN

LEXA

*L*ater that night, Lexa lay in bed, staring up at the elaborate pictures of the sea and beaches painted on the ceiling of her room. She touched her lips. They tingled with the memory of Ryke's kisses. She kicked her legs with a squeal, ignoring the soreness from dancing all night.

Sneaking around with Ryke in the gardens gave her a thrill that not even a tsunami wave could have achieved. It ignited a fire she never knew existed inside of her. Now the flame was alight. It had awakened a desire that could not be tamed.

She wondered how long it would be before she could see Ryke again and if the King would agree to a different arrangement. Could they really be together?

That morning, she thought there was no way she could end up with the man she truly loved or find her father without agreeing to a loveless marriage. But now Ryke had given her hope that not only would she get her father back, but she would be able to be with her one true love.

She bit her lip and wriggled further under the covers with another squeal. She could still taste him on her tongue, and she wrapped her arms around herself in a bid to erase the hollow feeling of missing him.

A knock on the door had her sitting up in bed with her heart racing. The maids had already left for the night and weren't supposed to return until sunrise. She held her breath, straining her ears, but couldn't hear anything.

She wondered if perhaps she had imagined the sound. Nonetheless, she swung her legs out of bed and tiptoed barefoot across the moonlit room to the closed door.

"Lexa," a hushed voice spoke through the door.

Ryke.

Lexa sucked in a breath, her hand hovering

over the brass door handle. She caught her reflection in the mirror and glanced at her sheer nightgown, leaving very little to the imagination, and her long hair tied loosely, hanging over her shoulder.

"Are you awake?"

Lexa pulled her hair free and dragged her fingers through it. She pulled it over both shoulders to cover herself in an attempt to offer a little more modesty before yanking the door open.

Before she could register what was happening, Ryke jumped into the room and shut the door behind him, pressing his back against it.

She watched him for a moment. The dim light of the moon cast shadows over his face. Then his eyes met hers before traveling down her body. The heat of his stare lit up all sorts of areas inside her. She licked her dry lips in anticipation.

Ryke shook his head as though to erase a forbidden thought. "I'm leaving."

"Leaving?" Her eyes followed him as he walked farther into the room. "Where are you going?"

He halted with his back to her and dragged a hand over his chin. "I'm going to save your father, but I have to leave tonight. And I'll do it demanding nothing in return." He turned around, his eyes shining in the bright moonlight. "You shouldn't be forced into a marriage just so you can get your father back."

"I'll come with you," Lexa said, stepping forward, but she stopped when Ryke shook his head.

"No. It's too dangerous. I've already assembled a crew I can trust. You stay here where I know you'll be safe."

"I don't want you to go alone. It's too dangerous for you too," she insisted. But Ryke took her face in his hand and caressed her cheek with his thumb, his eyes lingering on her.

"There isn't a risk I wouldn't take for you," he said, his deep voice making her insides vibrate. "And no danger I wouldn't face."

Lexa bit her lip and found Ryke's collar. She gripped the cotton material and pulled him to her. Without resistance, Ryke greedily captured her mouth in a kiss and slid his tongue over her bottom lip in a way that made Lexa weak at the knees.

It took a moment for Lexa to realize he'd slowly been backing her up, and she sucked in a breath when her back hit the wall. She welcomed the pressure of his body against hers, and the contact prompted an agonized groan to rip from Ryke's throat. In one swift motion, he picked her up, and she hitched up her nightdress to allow her legs to wrap around him.

Heat radiated throughout Lexa's body and her back arched as Ryke left a trail of rough kisses down her neck. His stubble grazed her skin in such a tantalizing way, she longed for him to kiss her everywhere, all night long.

After a few more kisses, his thigh pressed between hers as he braced her against the wall. Moaning, she threw back her head and bared her neck for his mouth as she draped her hands over his shoulders.

Ryke tore his lips from her collarbone to look deeply into her eyes. She held his gaze, smoothing down his hair over his ear while his chest kept her pinned to the wall.

A deep longing stirred inside of her, and a bubble of emotion rose to her chest.

"Please don't leave me here," she begged. "I cannot part from you again. I cannot bear it."

Ryke carried her across the room, and in the blink of an eye, she was lying on the bed with him on top of her. She sucked in a breath, and he caught her gasp with his mouth. He kissed her until her worries scattered. She arched her back, tangling her legs in the sheets as he moved above her. He kissed her roughly and with rising passion as her nightgown came undone and her hair sprayed over the bed. That was the closest she felt to freedom since she left the sea. And though Ryke's hungry eyes looked at her like she was bare, she was still wearing more clothing than she was used to.

His hand slid up her thigh, caressing her bare skin, and she could feel the rough edges of his calluses. He was a man who worked with his hands, and the strength and hardness in them lit her ablaze. Her skin heated under his touch, and she pulled up on the bottom of his cotton shirt with lustful curiosity. His ab muscles tightened when her palms skimmed over them, and he brushed his mouth over hers. Lexa caught his bottom lip between her teeth and chuckled when he moaned. Then he kissed her, his tongue dancing over hers until she relaxed against his body. Ryke kissed with just the right blend of softness and hunger, and she thought she could happily spend the rest of the night just tasting his lips.

Lexa lost all sense of reason as she succumbed to the thrill of the moment. What if someone happened to walk past her room, would they hear the bedframe knocking against the wall? Or Ryke's soft grunts along with her moans as she allowed him to devour her like she was a delightful dessert?

If they got caught, Lexa could only imagine the trouble they would be in.

"Lexa..." Her name came out in a rough grunt, as if parting from her at that moment caused him physical pain.

"Don't say it," she whispered.

"I have to go." His hot breath tickled her cheek as he rested his forehead to hers and closed his eyes. "But I promise, I'll come back for you."

She opened her eyes to meet his. He smiled, and she reached up to caress his face. His stubble rough against the tip of her fingers. The same stubble that was just moments ago licking her skin. "I survived the death of my mother, the disappearance of my father, but I am certain that my heart would not bear losing you."

He pressed his lips to her forehead, then pulled back with a sigh. "Assure your heart, my dear," he said, peering into her eyes. "I will return. And when I do, I will never leave your side again."

He left a final peck on her forehead, then jumped from the bed. He gave her a wink, then reached for the door and closed it behind him.

When her breathing returned to normal, Lexa became aware of just how dry her mouth was. Living on the land made her extra thirsty, and she already had all the water Wendy left by her bed. She grabbed a shawl and covered herself, then ventured out of her room in search of the kitchen.

As she walked along the dark vacant halls, Lexa couldn't stop grinning, thinking about Ryke returning with her father, who would be so grateful he'd waive the law that mermaids and men couldn't breed, and the King of the Shores and the King of the Sea would agree to coexist in peace. Then Lexa and Ryke would marry, and everyone would live happily ever after.

Ryke being a pirate was only a minor detail her father would need to overlook.

Just as she was thinking about her happy ending, a strip of golden light beneath a door caught her attention. As she approached it, a low murmur grew louder. She tiptoed to the closed door, recognizing the voices to belong to the King and the Prince.

"Father, I can't go through with this. I don't want an arranged marriage. I want to marry for love."

"My son, you must look at the big picture here. Once you are united with the Princess of the Sea, we will be able to rule over both the land and the sea."

"But father, do I not deserve to be happy?"

"After the wedding, we'll ship her off to one of the castles further north. Then you will be free to court whomever you wish, and with the Princess gone, it will make it far easier for our men to hunt mermaids."

"Wait. What are you saying… you want to keep hunting mermaids?" the Prince asked, the shock in his voice clear as a bell.

Lexa held her breath and leaned closer to the door so as not to miss a single word.

The King gave a deep laugh. "The mermaids trust their princess. Lexa thinks we'll form a peace treaty, and the mermaids will believe it. But in actual fact, this marriage will enable us to hunt and sell more mermaids than ever. Lexa is the key to all of this, and she'll never see it coming."

Lexa stumbled back, the King's words hitting her like a thunderclap. She turned on her heels and staggered down the hall, her mind reeling. She could not stay at that castle a moment longer. It wasn't safe for her there.

She hurried back into her room with her heart racing, then pressed her back against the closed door. A strong longing to return to the sea overcame her, but she couldn't without her fin.

She took in a deep breath, willing her mind to think. Where else could she go?

Or better yet.

What would Atlantis expect from their queen?

CHAPTER ELEVEN

RYKE

*R*yke leaned over the galleon's railing and watched as the tip of the sun peeked over the horizon. The ship was already moving at full speed toward one of the most perilous journeys he'd ever set out to do. But despite the dangers, his heart was at ease.

His love for Lexa overshadowed his agitation. Even if he didn't make it back home alive, he had a document written before he left, stating that the only reward he sought was Lexa's freedom. She deserved to find love, even if not with him.

The cool breeze was salty as it brushed his face. He closed his eyes and thought about Lexa. The scent of her skin always smelled like an ocean breeze, and the memory brought his mind back to their secret meeting in the maze. Their farewell in her bedroom.

"Sir," one of his men called out from behind him. "Look what we found."

Ryke turned around to find two of his men holding the arms of two young women. It took his brain a few seconds to register their faces.

"Lexa? Wendy?" He staggered forward, shocked. "What are you two doing here?"

Lexa yanked herself free from the man's grip, then moved toward Ryke. "Your uncle," she said. "He doesn't just want a peace treaty. He wants to rule Atlantis and intensify his mermaid hunting."

"What?" Ryke shook his head. "How did you come upon such information?"

Lexa pulled Ryke to the front of the ship where they could be alone, then lowered her voice. "I overheard him talking to your cousin last night," she went on. "He wants to use my title as princess to gain my people's trust, then ship me off to the Northern Kingdom."

Ryke ran a hand through his black hair, his mind spinning. How could his uncle be capable of such a wicked scheme? Though what shocked him most was that his cousin was going along with it. Lexa was right in not staying in the castle, but it was still too dangerous for her on the ship.

"What about returning to sea?" Ryke suggested. "You will be safer in Atlantis."

"I can't. In order to shift back into my mermaid form, I would have to break this." She touched her necklace. "If I do that, I'll lose my legs, and…" Her gaze softened as she touched his face. "I'm not ready to leave this world yet."

He kissed her hand. He wasn't ready to lose her either, but taking her with him made him nervous. He had no idea what enemies he would come across or what dangers he would face, and keeping her safe was all that mattered to him.

He shook his head, clearing his thoughts, then pulled her into his arms and kissed her forehead. "We'll figure something out. Now, let's get you something to eat. You must be famished."

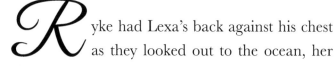

yke had Lexa's back against his chest as they looked out to the ocean, her long black hair flowing in the wind. She sucked in a deep breath as if the ocean was somehow comforting her.

"A shell for your thoughts?" Ryke whispered, his voice gentle in her ear.

Lexa's chuckle was weak, then she sighed. "The last time I spoke with my father, we argued. I called him a hypocrite."

Ryke couldn't even imagine the guilt and regret that must've been festering inside her precious heart. He wrapped an arm around her, and she reached for him. "Why not think about what you will say to him when you see him again?"

She let out a long breath. "He grieved my mother's death by escaping to the Chanted Forest and having a child with a human woman. What exactly do you say to that?"

Ryke shook his head as if he hadn't heard her correctly. He opened his mouth to say something, but found no words. She was right; what could one say to that? He nuzzled her hair, pressing his lips to the top of her head. "I'm sorry to hear about your mother."

He could feel her body relax against his chest,

and being able to soothe her, even in a small way, made him feel good.

"She lost her voice," Lexa said, leaning her head back against his shoulder. "When a mermaid loses their voice, they die quicker. It's a form of terminal illness in our world, which is ironic because mermaid scales have some of the most powerful healing properties known to men."

"How did she lose her voice?" Ryke asked.

He could feel Lexa's shoulder tense against him. "She made a deal with a sea creature named Neri."

"What kind of deal?"

Lexa shook her head. "I don't know. She never told me, and neither did my father." Suddenly, Lexa swung around with her eyes wide. "That's it. That's what I'll ask when I see him again." Then her eyes darkened just a little. "Right after I tell him that his daughter, the Princess of the Sea, has fallen head over heels over a *pirate*."

Ryke winced despite the playful gleam having returned to her eyes. "If your father doesn't kill me for falling for you, I am certain he will kill me for bringing you along."

She laughed and threw her arms around

Ryke's neck. "The way I see it, if I save my father, I will owe nothing to the King of the Shores. So, I had to come. For the sake of my own freedom."

That was a valid point, but the thought of Lexa running head-on into danger made his stomach churn. "These pirates aren't like the others."

"And?" She narrowed her eyes, unafraid. "I may have legs, but don't forget, I'm a mermaid. I'm a pirate's worst nightmare."

And a ravishing one at that, he couldn't help but think. Forgetting all about the topic at hand, a mischievous smile spread across his face. "To one particular pirate, though, I would say you're quite a dream."

He pulled her into his arms, and she suppressed a smile. "I'm trying to be serious here, you know?"

"Oh, I know," he said, his eyes falling to her lips. "But since, clearly, there's no going back, I figured I might as well make the best of the situation, wouldn't you agree?"

"I believe so." She lowered her eyes to the hand that was fidgeting with his shirt. "What do you have in mind?"

He leaned into her ear. "We could push each

other to our limits?"

Her eyes darkened as an intrigued smile spread across her face. "Go on."

Flashing a crooked smile, Ryke stepped back and drew his sword. "Have you ever used one of these?"

The clanging of swords echoed in the wind as Lexa swung hers to strike against Ryke's. He stepped back as Lexa moved forward, slashing the air with a succession of lunges. He blocked her strikes and smirked at the flash behind Lexa's eyes. She moved with grace and poise, handling her weapon like it was an extension of her body. He had to admit, she was good for a beginner.

But not good enough.

He pressed the length of his blade against hers and rotated it until the sword slipped from her hands. He kicked it across the deck with a grin, then pinned her against the wooden beam with his body. "You're getting better."

"I already told you," Lexa said, looking at him

with an expression both fierce and gentle. "I don't need a sword to win a fight."

"It's still good to have options."

Lexa gave him a skeptical look. "Are you sure you're not just saying that so you can keep pressing up against me?"

Ryke smiled as her heaving chest sent ripples of pleasure through him. "That is definitely a perk."

The playful sound of a dolphin came from a distance, and Lexa's eyes sparkled with excitement. "Jinko!" she said, turning toward the sound.

Ryke stepped back, releasing Lexa. "Who?"

She hurried to lean over the side of the boat with a broad grin. "Jinko!"

Ryke joined her and leaned over the wooden railing to see what Lexa was looking at. What he saw, though, was the oddest sight. A dolphin jumped next to the ship with a small red lobster holding onto its fin.

"Bob! Hackett!" Lexa's smile grew even wider, watching as a seagull swooped down and grabbed the lobster from the dolphin's head. He flew upward and dropped the lobster on the railing next to Lexa.

"Oh, boys…" Lexa scooped up the lobster in

her hands and twirled around as if she was waltzing with the shelled creature. "I can't believe you're here!"

The lobster, who seemed to have been named Bob, started to make a screaming noise Ryke had never heard before. He sounded like an angry parent, and if he had eyebrows, they would probably be furrowed as he seemed to have been scolding her.

But Lexa didn't seem to take him seriously. She simply continued to waltz with him, just as Ryke had taught her the night of the ball.

"I missed you so much, Bob!"

Ryke watched her with amusement. She was a fast learner.

Whether Lexa did it on purpose or not, Ryke wasn't sure, but when she threw the lobster in the air, the angry sounds came to a halt. His eyes, Ryke could swear, stretched wide in panic moments before the seagull circled around and caught him in the air.

Lexa's slender shoulders trembled as she let out a melodic laugh, leaning over the railing again. The seagull dropped the quiet lobster next to her again as she waved at the dolphin.

Jinko, which seemed to have been the dolphin,

jumped up from the water and twirled in the air, waterdrops cascading off its body in a display of glittering wonder. And as the dolphin flipped again, it launched streams of water in all directions. It blated again as if showing off to Lexa. She beamed.

Ryke watched the dolphin for a moment, only then realizing that must have been the same dolphin who had taken him back to the marina. Ryke couldn't help but wonder if taking him away from the island was the dolphin's way of helping Ryke to survive or getting him away from Lexa.

"Wait, what?" Lexa swung around to face the seagull with her brows furrowed. "Where?"

The seagull made a noise that almost sounded like a warning call. Though Ryke had no idea what was happening, Lexa seemed concerned.

"What's wrong?" Ryke asked, drawing closer to her.

She turned to Ryke, alarmed.

"Sir!" One of his men yelled from the top of the lookout post. Ryke turned to the bow of the ship just as it headed straight into a cloud of thick fog. Everyone fell silent as they sailed through swirling cold mist so dense, Ryke could hardly see two feet in front of him. As though they entered a bubble, the sounds of faraway birds and rushing waters faded. Then, an eerie silence made the hairs on the back of Ryke's neck stand on end.

As they emerged on the other side, a large galleon appeared bobbing in the water ahead of them. And before anyone could take another breath, an ear-splitting boom filled the air, followed by the succession of gunfire.

"Pirates!" Ryke bellowed.

All of his men were jolted to action. They scrambled to retrieve their weapons and load their pistols. The crew hurriedly got into position at the port side of the ship and aimed their pistols, ready to fire. Ryke ran through a shower of bullets, then climbed the ladder and grabbed the helm. He gritted his teeth and yanked on it with all his strength, turning it as far as it would go. The wood creaked with the sharp turn, and the front of the ship scraped the enemy's galleon.

Gunfire exploded, and Ryke ducked behind the helm.

"Take control!" He ordered one of his men to take his place, then ran toward the railing, pulling out his pistol. He took cover as he shot at the pirates' ship.

The pirates let out angry war cries that

sounded like a mixture between roars and screams. Ryke was on high alert, his body flooded with adrenaline, and he loaded the barrel of his pistol as a torrent of bullets rained over him.

But then he caught Lexa jumping up on the railing and holding onto a wooden beam as if she was about to jump off the ship. Her light cotton dress flapped in the wind as she stood with such fearless confidence. For a moment, Ryke was frozen, and judging by the pause in the gunfire, he was not the only one. But then he came to his senses and shook his head.

"Lexa!" Ryke ran toward her as the gunfire resumed once more. "Get down! Take cover! Lexa!"

Her voice rose above the chaos and the gunfire ceased. The sweet melody that came from her lips was the most entrancing sound he'd ever heard. The words she sang held resonance in his heart, and like an invisible force taking over his body, a warmth spread from head to toe. Suddenly, the pirates vanished from view, and all Ryke could do was listen to the words flowing from Lexa's mouth in the form of a most delightful melody.

Still and quiet, always. Fill our hearts with wonder. Never knowing pain or sorrow.

Ryke fell to his knees on the deck, staring at Lexa in amazement as her voice rose louder, sending gentle vibrations into the air as if she were singing to the heavens. She met his eyes briefly before directing her voice at the enemy's ship, and Ryke regained his senses. He staggered forward and peeked over the railing.

The pirates on the galleon, slowly, one by one, began coming out of hiding to watch Lexa perform just for them. They stared at her in a daze. But then they jumped in the water as if sacrificing themselves.

When the ships drew near, she walked across a wooden plank, still singing, her beautiful voice carried in the wind. Ryke followed after her as she jumped onto the enemy's galleon.

As she stood in the center of their ship, every male in the crew stared at her in a daze. Ryke jumped onto the enemy's ship and watched as she stopped in front of the captain.

One look at her and the captain's eyes went blank. His stare was empty as if hypnotized.

"I need your help," Lexa spoke in a gentle tone.

"What can we do for you?" the captain asked without hesitation.

"Tell me about Poseidon," she demanded. "Who took him?"

"We were offered the job," he confessed, his eyes still blank. "But we turned it down. We did not wish to engage Poseidon's wrath."

"Do you know who took him?"

"No."

Lexa stiffened, and Ryke knew she was bitterly disappointed. He was just about to comfort her, but the captain was not done.

"But I know where they would have taken him," the captain added, capturing Lexa's attention again.

"Where?" she demanded.

The captain was quiet for a moment, his eyes no longer blank, but instead, watching Lexa as if she were a rising sun. Ryke couldn't blame the man, but he didn't like anyone looking at her with such desire.

"Where?" she asked again.

The captain smiled as if a peaceful wave washed over him. "Neverland."

Lexa bowed her head. "Thank you for your cooperation, Captain."

She turned on her heels and flashed Ryke a smug smile. "See..." she said, walking past him. "I don't need a sword to win a fight."

CHAPTER TWELVE

LEXA

I *don't like this,* Bob said, clinging onto the railing like his little life depended on it. Lexa ignored him as she drummed her fingernails on a post and looked wistfully into the dense fog.

They had sailed through endless clouds of gray for many hours, and the waters rocked the ship so much, half of the sailors got sick.

Lexa looked up at Ryke, standing by the helm. Every few minutes, he opened his brass spyglass and inspected their surroundings. The encasing thick fog made it of little use, but they could never be too careful.

I have a bad feeling about this. I feel it in my bones, Bob said, his claws snapping.

Lexa sighed. *You always have a bad feeling. Besides, there's no turning back now.*

She picked up a sword Ryke had given her and began to sharpen the weapon just so that she had something to do with the nervous energy in her hands. *I know what you're going to say, but, Bob, they're just rumors.*

Hackett stopped eating the scraps and joined Lexa on the deck. *Rumors about Neverland, you say? Why yes, I do believe I've heard a few.*

Bob looked from Lexa to Hackett and scuttled down the side of the ship to stand in front of Lexa's blade, giving her a steely glare.

Neverland, Neverland, ere winter she'll never know. Neverland, Neverland, young and fertile waters flow. Come to me in Neverland, come and be free. Bring your worries and labors with thee. Neverland, Neverland, ere winter we'll never know.

Bob stopped singing while Lexa suppressed a laugh. *That was beautiful, I had no idea you had such a lovely voice.*

Bob snapped his claws. *It's not supposed to be beautiful. It's a warning. You know what they say. Those who venture to Neverland do not return.*

Hackett ruffled his feathers with a honk. *That is true, I have heard that as well.*

Lexa dropped the metal with a huff and looked at the seagull hard. *And what would you have me do? Forget about my father?* She glared at Bob as well. *You are his most trusted advisor. Are you advising me to abandon your king?*

Bob did not reply, and before he could come up with an argument, Hackett soared into the sky above their heads and let out a warning cry.

We're approaching land!

Shortly after, Ryke yelled at his men to drop the anchor. "We'll take the boats from here."

Lexa jumped to her feet, then pulled her hair back into a ponytail. The sailors marched about, busying themselves with their tasks, some of them more eager to get off the ship than others. There was a violent judder followed by a splash, and the ship lurched to a halt. Ryke scaled the ladder and called out orders to his crew.

Lexa turned to Bob and Hackett. *Stay here until we return.* When Bob started to argue, she gave him a hard look. *You're safer on the ship. Besides, we shouldn't be long.*

Begrudgingly, Bob plopped down on the wooden floor. Meanwhile, Hackett had returned to the scraps and began to help himself. Trust a seagull not to grasp the gravity of a situation.

Lexa supposed he was the only soul on the ship with an appetite.

Lexa threw her hair back and straightened her dress as Wendy came to stand next to her. The crew lowered the boats into the water, and Ryke jumped down from the upper deck with a broad grin.

"Ready to save your father?" He held out his hand for Lexa and helped her climb over the edge of the ship.

"Ready as I'll ever be," she replied, climbing down the rope ladder with Wendy following close behind.

The crew sailed on small rowing boats through the misty fog, following the birds that flew ahead toward something that no human eye could see.

Lexa wrapped a shawl around her shoulders, hoping that they would get out of the fog soon. Its cool vapor licked her body like melting ice and made her shudder.

Then peaks of sunlight streamed through the fog and grew brighter, burning the mist away. Finally, the air cleared just enough for them to see a mountainous island. Lexa and Ryke looked up and marveled at the sheer size of it.

The green mountain was so tall it disappeared into the clouds high in the sky, and it appeared to be covered in trees or moss. Birds circled the trees, and a rainbow arched proudly from the waters to the mountains.

"Well, call me foolhardy, but I never thought I'd live to see the fabled Neverland with my own eyes," Ryke said, lowering his voice to a murmur.

They docked their boats on the sandy shores of Neverland, and Lexa helped Wendy out as she looked up, her eyes wide and shining with admiration.

"Be on your guard, we don't know who or what we'll be up against here," Ryke warned them as they walked toward the edge of a forest.

The salty sea breeze brushed Lexa's back, and the scent of pinecones had her feeling oddly relaxed.

Suddenly, Wendy grabbed her arm and pointed. *Tracks. They were dragging something heavy… in a net.*

Lexa eyed the grooves in the sand—they were headed straight for the woodland. "Wendy's right, look at those markings."

Ryke followed her line of sight and gave a firm nod. "Guns at the ready, men. I have no tolerance for whatever beast has stolen Poseidon."

They walked through the thick woodland for hours until their flasks had long been emptied and the searing sunshine beamed through the leaves of the trees above. A collection of sweat gathered on Lexa's temples, and her tongue was dry. It seemed like it had been days since her last drink.

"We're walking round in circles," one of the men complained.

Wendy shook her head, then pointed up a small trail. *This way.*

Lexa wasn't sure how Wendy knew where to go, but she trusted her more than the disgruntled sailors who now complained about their aches and pains and questioned their direction. Ryke frowned, his brows knitted together as he considered their next move. He chose to follow Wendy.

They trudged along a winding path up the mountainous island, and Lexa's legs grew heavier by the second. Soon, the crew stopped complaining and grew eerily quiet. Meanwhile, a symphony of birdsong filled the air, and the sunshine sparkled like glitter on the dirt paths.

The sound of rushing water caught Lexa's attention. She was not the only one to notice because soon the whole group began to veer off the path, following the sound. Ryke hacked through an overgrown bush and paved the way for the rest of them to file out into a clearing that led to a waterfall.

Lexa dropped to her knees and scooped crystal-clear water in her hands. She slurped it up without even caring how unladylike it must have looked to the others. But no one commented. Everyone took haste to quench their dying thirst, and before long, everyone was on their feet with beaming smiles and eyes sparkling again.

At first, Lexa was rejuvenated and glowing, but then her vision grew blurred, and the world shifted sideways as she staggered forward. Ryke asked her a question, but his voice sounded like a distant bell instead of actual words.

"I don't feel…" Lexa's tongue flopped helplessly in her mouth, and she collapsed to her knees. The others also fell on the ground and, one by one, all of them were lying down.

Lexa's cheek pressed against the dirt as she panted, wondering why she was so dizzy and lethargic. Then an impossibly strong wave of sleepiness washed over her, and before she knew it, she was out.

*W*hen Lexa woke up, she blinked into the sunlight and rubbed her eyes. Startled, she looked at her hands. They were softer than she'd ever known.

"What in the blazing stars happened to my beard?" one of the sailors said. Lexa looked at a young man who had the gruff voice of a fifty-year-old. He rubbed his baby-smooth chin and frowned.

As everyone else woke up, Lexa looked around and gasped. She was lying among a group of teens, who strangely resembled Ryke's crew. A young man with dark messy hair and a hook for his right hand stood over her. When her eyes took focus, she realized it was a younger version of Ryke, as if he had reversed the aging process by a few years. Not a worry line in sight. Only Wendy did not seem to have changed, considering she was already the youngest of the group to begin with.

"We're all younger," Lexa said, rising to her feet. She inspected her thin arms and rolled her shoulders, noticing how limber and supple she was. One of the other sailors seemed to have the same thoughts as he started doing lunges.

"Good heavens, my knees haven't felt this good since I was nineteen years old."

Ryke rubbed the back of his neck and frowned as he marched to the waterfall again. "What is this place?"

Lexa gasped as the memory of Bob's singing flooded her mind.

"Neverland, Neverland, ere winter she'll never know. Neverland, Neverland, young and fertile waters flow. Come to me in Neverland, come and be free. Bring your worries and labors with thee. Neverland, Neverland, ere winter we'll never know."

"What is that?" Ryke asked, walking toward her.

"A song about Neverland. You haven't heard it before?"

Young and fertile waters flow, Wendy cut in as she had been reading Lexa's lips. *Lexa, the water rejuvenated all of us.*

Lexa nodded. "Wendy says it was the water. That's what made us young again."

One of the sailors walked to the edge of the glittering water with his mouth hanging open.

"Captain Hook, can you imagine the riches we would get if we took some of this home?"

Ryke held up a hand and shook his head. "No one takes anything until we know exactly what this place is, and what it will do to us."

His voice echoed in the treetops, and birds flew out of the bushes and soared into the sky.

Ryke gave Lexa a nod. "We are here for one mission. To find King Poseidon. Let's stay focused."

The group was just getting ready to continue their journey when they were interrupted by a shower of squeals that ended with crackles and pops. Sparks flew, and a succession of bangs had the crew scatter in panic.

"We're under fire!"

"They're everywhere. Run for your lives!"

Before Ryke could rally them, the crew fled into the woods in all directions, leaving Ryke, Lexa, and Wendy behind.

More squeals filled the air, followed by ear-splitting bangs. Lexa watched a spark whizz by, narrowly missing her ear, and looked at Wendy, who was holding her hand on the ground as though communicating with the earth. Then she turned to Lexa. *They are just boys.*

Before Lexa could ask what she meant, a group of young boys emerged from the trees with firecrackers in their hands. Many of them looked no older than fourteen, and the small one on the end looked like he had barely seven years on him.

The boys closed in on them, but Wendy jerked her head to the side, her eyes focused, and Lexa knew she sensed something. Or perhaps, *someone.*

Wendy raced to the left.

"Come on!" Lexa shouted to Ryke. The two of them dodged more firecrackers, and Lexa tried to ignore the war cries from the boys as they chased them deeper into the woods.

Branches and thick tree roots slowed them down as they ambled their way through the overgrowth. Ryke raced upfront and slashed through the jungle with his hook, but they couldn't move fast enough. The boys were catching up, and Lexa wasn't sure what these children were capable of. Or whether they were really just boys. Perhaps they drank the water too, and really, they're menacing pirates who had stumbled upon the island in times past.

Just then, a twig snapped on the ground, and a huge net scooped Lexa, Wendy, and Ryke up into the trees.

The boys circled the ground beneath the swinging net and shouted with glee as they danced about and threw their hands in the air.

But then a flash of golden light shot through the clearing, and the boys fell quiet.

"Oh no, it's Tink," one of the boys said, his voice disappointed.

Another flash of golden light hit one of the boys like a zap. He clutched his buttocks with both hands and ran screaming into the woods.

"Come on, Tinkerbell. We're only having fun!" one of the older boys said.

Lexa watched a trail of light darting all around the boys and zapping each one until they all promptly ran in different directions. Soon, they were alone, and Lexa held her breath, wondering if they too were going to be under attack.

The light flew above their heads, and with a crack, the rope snapped, sending Ryke, Wendy, and Lexa tumbling to the ground.

Lexa dusted herself off and they got back to their feet as the golden light floated down to their eye level. It was only then that Lexa could see a small fairy encased by the golden light.

Lexa squinted. The fairy was like a tiny human, no bigger than the palm of Lexa's hand.

It was a woman wearing a leaf as a dress and ginger hair tied into a bun.

"Thank you for saving us. Are you Tinkerbell?" Lexa asked, looking at the fairy with curiosity.

The fairy opened her tiny mouth, and all that came out was a succession of squeaks. Ryke scratched his head, and Wendy looked puzzled, clearly neither of them able to interpret.

Then a voice entered Lexa's mind. *I am Tinkerbell, guardian of Neverland. And none of you are safe as long as you stay here.*

Before Lexa could relay the message, Tinkerbell zoomed into the tree line, and Wendy bolted after her.

"Where is she going?" Ryke asked.

"I don't know, but if we don't hurry up, we'll lose them!" Lexa shouted as they both broke into a sprint.

Wendy crossed the jungle like a cat, bounding off of tree trunks, swinging from vines and hopping over uprooted trees with so much ease, Lexa wondered if she had done this before. There was something instinctual by the way Wendy tore through the woods, and it took all of Lexa's concentration and energy to keep up.

Ryke grumbled, "Slow down," a few times, his breath coming out in raspy coughs. But Wendy did not slow down. Finally, they stumbled out of the jungle onto the sand, and for a gleeful moment, Lexa wanted to dive into the glittering sea and take a deep breath of aqua, rehydrating her body again.

Tinkerbell hovered in the air and squeaked again, the noises were sharp and quick, like a bee having a fight with a wasp. *You must leave, right now. You escaped death once today, but if Pan finds you, you will not be so lucky to escape it again.*

"Pan?" Ryke asked, echoing Lexa, who had relayed the message. "Peter Pan?"

"You've heard of him?" Lexa asked.

Ryke frowned, pacing the sand. "Only rumors." He walked up to Tinkerbell. "We have reason to believe that King Poseidon is here, and we're not leaving without him."

Tinkerbell flew to Ryke's ear, and as Lexa leaned in, she could just make out the squeaky voice, though it seemed that Tinkerbell was screaming at the top of her lungs.

"Forget about him. Leave now and don't come back. If Pan catches you, there is no telling what monstrous fate beholds you!"

Lexa's heart sank. Tinkerbell didn't argue that her father was not in Neverland, which meant he was most likely there. She couldn't just leave. Not now. Even if they had to risk crossing paths with this mysterious enemy named Pan.

"No," Ryke said, his voice firm and hand clenched into a fist. "My crew is on this island, and I have no intention of leaving them."

He began to march back toward the forest, and Tinkerbell flew like an angry bee around their heads.

"You're making a huge mistake! Turn back now!"

Lexa exchanged looks with Wendy, and they nodded in agreement. When it was clear that no one was leaving, Tinkerbell made a final squeak, then zoomed back into the trees. Lexa turned to Wendy and Ryke. "She said, 'your funeral.'"

Ryke halted and turned to face them, his expression fierce and determined.

"I don't care what she said. I never leave a man behind."

Then he turned around and disappeared into the jungle.

CHAPTER THIRTEEN

RYKE

*H*ours passed by until the jungle was blanketed in darkness, except for the soft silver glow of moonlight through the gaps in the trees above their heads. Ryke charged forward, cutting down overgrowth with his hook and snapping twigs underfoot. It had been a long day, and his muscles screamed for rest, but the beating drum of his heartbeat in his ears urged him forward.

Owls hooted in the distance, and the gentle roar of the ocean floated through the jungle like a breath. If it wasn't for Ryke's heart hammering in his chest, he might have thought the night was still and tranquil.

A sudden chill filled the air, and as a cold

breeze blew, it whistled like a bird, warning them to turn around and go back to the ship. Despite the rising hairs on the back of Ryke's neck, he pressed on. As he already told Tinkerbell, he was not one to leave men behind.

The scent of burning wood stopped Ryke in his tracks, and he moved his head, trying to locate the direction of the fire. "This way," he said to Lexa and Wendy, who followed close behind him.

Ryke unsheathed his sword to cut branches that hung low, blocking their path, but just as he was about to swing his blade once more, Lexa touched his arm and lifted a finger to her lips to shush him.

He blinked at her, wondering what she had heard. She closed her eyes as if straining her ears for a distant sound. "Do you hear that?" she whispered, shooting her eyes open with alarm.

"What, the birds?" Ryke asked.

Lexa shook her head. "Those aren't birds. They're whistles."

Lexa darted down the hill, swerving the trees like a gazelle. Ryke ran to keep up, with Wendy by his side. By the time they reached a lake, Lexa was already midway through it, the water up to her waist.

He wanted to call out to her, to tell her to turn around. Ryke knew nothing about that island, or those waters, but the whistling had grown louder and the burning smell stronger. They were close, and Ryke was afraid he would be heard.

Wendy hopped onto a rock near the edge and wobbled. Ryke offered her his arm, and she took it. He stepped into the water, and his boots sank into the muddy ground, getting soaked within seconds. Despite not liking the sensation, he pushed forward.

Now there were no trees above them. The moon was bright, and the reflected stars looked like they were floating just above the surface of the murky water.

He descended the slippery slope underwater until his lower body was completely covered. When the ground finally leveled, water was up to his waist. He looked at Lexa ahead of him, and the water was just below the chest. As he followed her, his boots slid across slimy leaves, and it took every ounce of focus to keep his balance and support Wendy.

He took another step forward, but a tug on his arm had him looking back with confusion. Wendy hadn't jumped onto the next rock. Instead, she looked ahead with all blood drained from her face. Her eyes were wide as she stared into the dark water at what would have been her next stepping-stone.

Ryke wondered if she was concerned about the size of the jump, he gave her hand a reassuring squeeze and tugged on it lightly. But her panicked eyes flickered toward him.

"What?" he mouthed to her, knowing she could read his lips.

She shook her head, and that was when he realized what she was trying to say. His eyes slowly moved toward the stepping-stone, which was not a stone at all. The bright moon above allowed him to see pattern ridges where it was supposed to have been smooth. And the tiny ripples around it indicated that although it wasn't moving, it was definitely bobbing in the water.

"Lexa, stop moving," he whispered loud enough for her to hear.

She stopped and turned around.

"I said *don't move*," he repeated, scanning around the lake, suddenly realizing those shiny diamonds were not a reflection of the stars. They were eyes.

And when the textured stone began to move,

Ryke spotted the spiked tail slinking behind. His stomach churned, and he stopped breathing as his eyes turned slowly toward Lexa.

"They're crocodiles," he whispered. She suppressed a gasp.

The creature swam with its tail weaving on the surface of the water. He turned around, and Ryke spotted his eyes turning in Lexa's direction.

"You speak to animals, don't you?" Ryke asked.

Lexa nodded.

"Do they know we're here?"

"Yes."

"What are they saying?"

Lexa was silent for a moment. "You don't want to know."

Ryke watched the creature swim slowly toward Lexa. "I'm guessing they're not friendly, then?"

Lexa shook her head. "Not at all. And they hate mermaids, for some reason."

"What do they want?" Though, by the fear in Lexa's eyes, he knew the answer.

"Dinner."

The creature darted toward Lexa. Ryke jumped forward and buried his hook into the crocodile's tail before he could reach her. The animal growled in pain, snapped its lethal jaws, then bared its razor-sharp teeth toward Ryke.

The reptile yanked its tail free, then whipped it around. It hit Wendy's leg and threw her off balance, sending her into the water with a yelp. Ryke grabbed onto her and pulled her toward him. She gasped, spitting out the dirty water from her mouth. The glittering eyes of the predator zeroed in on Ryke. He pushed Wendy behind him and pulled out his knife.

As he was about to swing, a mermaid fin broke through the surface of the water, its iridescent scales glowing in the moonlight. The lake began glowing blue as sapphire, and when Ryke looked down, he spotted the glow coming from the plants below.

The creature dove underwater, and Wendy dug her fingers into Ryke's arm, pinching his skin. But there was too much adrenaline charging through his body to feel any pain. He gripped the knife, ready to strike, his heart racing in his chest.

The fin pushed Ryke and Wendy back, then slapped the crocodile in the face. It backed away from the blue glow as if it were deadly. And when

Ryke looked around, the rest of the hungry eyes had disappeared.

The mermaid swam back and bobbed in front of them. Her scales glowed the same electric blue as the plants below. Her red curls swirled over her shoulders. Wendy let out a long breath of relief, but Ryke kept his grip on his knife, his shoulders still tense. Though Lexa loved him, all other mermaids still hated pirates. He wouldn't be surprised if she grabbed him by his coat and drowned him right there.

"Remi?" Lexa swam back, pushing herself through the murky water. "Is that you?"

The mermaid swung around toward Lexa with wide eyes, then nodded. Lexa pulled her friend into a hug.

"What are you doing here?"

The mermaid opened her mouth to speak, but no sound came out.

Lexa's brows furrowed. "What happened to your voice?"

When the mermaid began to sign, a high pitch screech blared like a siren all over the island. The mermaid doubled over in pain and covered her ears. Ryke and Lexa did the same. To Ryke, the sound was so earsplitting he was sure his eardrums were going to burst.

Lexa pulled him underwater, muffling the siren. It eased the tension, but he could only hold his breath for so long. His lungs began to throb. He could still sense the vibrations of the screech on the glowing ground under his feet.

Just as his lungs were depleted of air, the mermaid signed to Lexa one last time, then swam away. Once she disappeared, the blaring screech came to a halt. Ryke stood, his face breaking the surface of the water with a giant gulp of air.

"What was that?" Ryke asked, though it was hard to even hear his own voice over the ringing in his ears.

Lexa shrugged, then turned to Wendy to make sure she was okay. When she stared at Ryke and Lexa with a puzzled look, as though she had no idea what had just happened, Lexa rested a hand on Wendy's shoulder with a sigh of relief. Thankfully, she wasn't affected by the torturous noise.

Ryke rubbed his ears as he followed Lexa out of the water. Gradually, his hearing returned, and he could hear the whistling a lot louder than before. They were getting closer. The smell of fire was also stronger as they continued on their way. As they made their way into the forest and up the hill, Ryke stripped off his leather coat and dropped it on the ground. It was extra heavy now that it was wet, and being unable to run as fast as he could was a disadvantage that could cost him his life.

"So, what happened to that mermaid's voice?" Ryke asked, picking up his pace to walk next to Lexa.

"I don't know," she replied. "She didn't get to say."

"What *did* she say?"

A puzzled crease formed between Lexa's brows. "Something about not singing."

"What does that even mean?"

"I don't know." Lexa shrugged. "She left before I could ask."

Once they reached the top of the hill, Lexa crouched behind a thick bush, pulling Ryke with her. Wendy followed.

"There they are," Lexa whispered.

Ryke used his hook to pull down a thick branch that was obscuring his vision. A group of wild boys whistled as they danced around a bonfire. They were the same ones they had run into earlier, joined by even more of them.

"Look, over there!" Lexa whispered, pointing to the trees beyond the dancing group.

Four of Ryke's crewmen wrestled against thick ropes that tied them to tree trunks. Their struggle only stirred the boys to behave wilder and more excited.

"So, what's the plan?" Lexa asked in a low tone.

"We'll sneak up from behind and cut my men free," Ryke suggested.

"But then what? Even with your crew released, we'll still be outnumbered."

Ryke scanned the campsite. There must've been about ten wild boys dancing around the fire. And that wasn't even counting the boys swinging on hammocks above the trees, whistling. Lexa was right. Even if he did release his men, they would still be outnumbered.

Wendy gasped, and Ryke's eyes darted back to the wild boys. Another young man with ginger hair arrived, but instead of joining the wild boys' dancing, he swaggered in front of Ryke's men.

"What have we got here?" the young man

asked, and the wild boys got even wilder, cele-
brating the young man's arrival.

What was so special about him? Ryke couldn't
tell.

"Do you know who that is?" Ryke asked
Wendy, and she watched his lips very carefully in
the dark.

Wendy nodded, then she turned to Lexa and
signed. Lexa's eyes widened.

"What?" Ryke asked.

Lexa stared at him. "That's Peter Pan."

"What is your business in Neverland?" Peter
asked, and the wild boys fell in hushed silence. He
paced in front of Ryke's men, giving each one a
steely look, but none of them answered. "What's
the matter, fairies got your tongue?"

Ryke's men looked at one another in fear but
still didn't respond.

"Oh, I see. You're loyal to your captain." Peter
crossed his arms. "That's very admirable. Really.
So, how about we try this a different way?" He
narrowed his eyes as a wicked smile spread across
his face. "Let's play a game, shall we?"

The wild boys cheered, then began dancing
around the fire again.

"Take that one," Peter ordered.

A few of the wild boys grabbed one of the crew members and threw him on the ground. They encircled him, and after tying a rope to his feet, they tossed the rope over the thick tree branch above.

"Hang him up!" Peter commanded, and three wild boys grabbed onto the rope and pulled.

Ryke's man grunted as he turned upside down, hung by his feet. And when he realized his head was above the burning bonfire, he panted with eyes wide and fearful.

Ryke jolted forward, but Lexa grabbed his shirt and pulled him back down. He ran a finger over his hook as if sharpening it.

Lexa dug her nails into Ryke's arm while suppressing a gasp. "Look!"

Ryke followed her gaze and spotted Wendy hiding behind one of the trees, cutting the rope and freeing the rest of the men.

Ryke touched his sheath. When had she taken his knife? And how did she get there so fast?

"I'm going to ask one more time," Peter said, pulling out his own blade from his sheath and looking up at the man hanging upside down. "What brought you all to Neverland?"

"Poseidon," the man said, his eyes shooting to the growing flames mere inches below.

"Who is looking for him?" Peter asked, flipping his knife between his fingers.

When the man hesitated, Peter signaled to one of the wild boys, and he lowered the sailor closer to the fire until it singed his hair.

The man began to weep. "His daughter! That's all I know. I swear! Please!"

Peter's eyes widened in surprise, then he looked around the clearing. Ryke grabbed Lexa, pulling her down and out of sight. Pan shifted his attention back to the sailor. "Poseidon's daughter is *here?*"

"Yes."

"Well, that wasn't part of the plan, but it sure is a pleasant surprise," Peter said, smiling at the hanging man. "Thank you for your help."

He grabbed his knife and tossed it with a simple flick of the wrist. The blade sliced through the air and struck the rope. It snapped, and the wild boys cheered, anticipating the man to set ablaze.

Ryke leaped forward and jumped over the fire, ramming his chest against the sailor, tackling him to the ground.

The wild boys fell silent and stared at Ryke as he rolled off his crewmate and checked if he was all right. He turned to see Peter looking toward the trees where the rest of the crew members had been tied. There was nothing but piles of broken rope on the ground. Wendy was also nowhere in sight.

"Get them!" Peter commanded.

The wild boys' battle cries filled the air as they took up their weapons. Ryke jumped to his feet, and his man rose with him. They were surrounded with makeshift spears and knives pointed at them.

Ryke pulled out his own sword. He might've been outnumbered, but he was not going down without a fight.

The wild boys screamed into the night as if sounding a warning call. Perhaps a warning to the forest that they were about to end a life. Peter stood across the fire with shadows dancing on his face. He watched Ryke with lethal eyes, as if the situation was somehow entertaining for him to watch.

Then a soft hum carried in the wind, and the wild boys fell silent. They dropped their weapons. Another gentle hum followed, and they looked at one another as if they were familiar with the sound. One of them smiled as if it was pleasant to his ears. Then, the humming turned into the sweetest melody, and when it grew louder, Ryke recognized it.

He spun around just as Lexa stepped into view. Her dark hair flowed back in the breeze and her piercing green eyes glowed with the reflection of the flames.

"Lexa, no!"

But she had already begun singing. Her voice rose above the chaos, and the wild boys dropped their weapons. Ryke fell to his knees, losing himself in the sweet melody that came from her lips. The sound lured him into a captivating bliss, and a warmth spread through his body.

Until her eyes came into focus, glowing greener than usual, and locked with his. His senses returned even though she was still singing, and it was as if she had loosened her hold on him, releasing him from the trance.

She turned to the wild boys once more. Their mouths hung open while their eyes were glazed over. Peter, on the other hand, smiled as if he was looking at a mountain of gold. He didn't have to say it. Ryke could tell by the sparkle in his eyes that he knew Lexa was the Princess of the Sea. And the way he eyed her like a forbidden treasure gave Ryke the urge to tear the smug smile off his face with his hook.

But most importantly, why wasn't Lexa's hypnosis working on him?

Suddenly, the sweet sound left Lexa's mouth, and she clutched her throat. The song was still playing as a glittering fog floated in the air. Ryke watched it rise, dancing with the wind. It traveled up toward the top of the trees as if it had been summoned by something or someone much more powerful.

As soon as the song ceased, the wild boys' eyes returned to their normal state, and they shook their heads in a daze. Lexa coughed as if she was choking.

Ryke turned to Pan with a deadly glare. "What have you done to her?"

Lexa continued to choke.

Ryke charged at Pan, but before he could get to him, Pan's feet left the ground, and he rose into the air like he was weightless.

Ryke slashed the air, only catching the bottom of Pan's shirt. "Get back down here, you coward, and fight me like a man!" Ryke barked.

Pan ignored Ryke's insults, and instead, kept his eyes fixed on Lexa, who stood across the camp with her eyes fluttering closed, looking like she was about to faint. When a wicked smile spread across Pan's face, Ryke darted toward Lexa.

Pan flew toward her and snatched her before she hit the ground. He swooped her up with him. Ryke tried to grab her, growling with fury, but only his fingertips brushed her leg before Pan flew her away, cackling with maniacal laughter.

"No!" Ryke yelled, watching Pan fly into the starry night with Lexa in his claws. "I'll get you for this, Pan!"

A war cry came from the darkened woods. Ryke turned toward the sound to find the rest of his crew members, charging toward the wild boys with thick branches as weapons.

The wild boys dropped their spears and staggered away, their minds still in a haze from Lexa's hypnosis.

Wendy emerged from the trees and approached Ryke, watching him with concern in her eyes. When she scanned around the camp, he knew she was looking for Lexa.

"Pan took her," Ryke hissed. "I swear, when I get my hook in him—"

Wendy touched Ryke's arm. She signed, but he didn't understand. His hand was shaking, his mind spinning. It was hard to focus.

Wendy sighed, then pointed to something in the distance.

Ryke squinted in the night. A dark statue sat at the top of a building far away. "What is that?" he murmured. Then his eyes adjusted, and he recognized the statues. "Are those mermaids?"

Wendy nodded.

Ryke turned to face her with renewed hope. "Is that where he's taking Lexa?"

Wendy nodded again.

Ryke picked up his sword from the ground and returned it to his sheath. "Let's go get that son of a siren."

CHAPTER FOURTEEN

LEXA

*W*histling wind slapped Lexa's cheeks as she came to her senses. Her head thumped and her ears rang as she looked around the world soaring past and tried to make sense of the situation. A vast lake shimmered below her dangling feet. An arm was clamped around her waist, and Lexa was careful not to move, but she caught sight of a flash of ginger hair and knew that Peter Pan was flying her away.

Where was he taking her?

Up ahead, poking out of the vast trees, stood a stone castle with gargoyle-like statues in the shape of alligators and mermaids on every turret. Lexa had a sense of foreboding looking at it, guessing that Peter must have been taking her there.

But judging by the way he was so callous with Ryke's crew, and would have gladly watched one burn alive, Lexa was not going to wait around and find out what dreadful fate he bestowed upon her.

She sucked in a deep breath, then jerked her elbow back, winding Pan just enough for him to grunt and lose his grip on her. Lexa free fell through the air, and for a few exhilarating moments, she knew what it felt like to be a seagull.

Then she crashed into a lake and fell like a boulder to the bottom of the murky waters. Lexa's pores soaked in the water like her body was taking a deep breath, reinvigorated. She swam effortlessly toward a bank, and a school of fish rushed past her, covering her in bubbles. *Swim away! Swim away! Death lies ahead,* a fish warned, his cries fading as they disappeared deeper into the lake.

Lexa waited for the bubbles to clear, and it took several moments for her to realize she wasn't breathing. Her chest screamed, a painful reminder that she was no longer a mermaid. In response, her legs kicked, and she burst through the surface of the water with a greedy gasp. There was little time to check if Peter had followed her, or to see where the current was taking her. Her lungs ached. The rushing sound of a waterfall flooded Lexa's senses, and before she could think straight, she got caught in a riptide and shot through the water and over the edge until she fell, seemingly forever.

Once she made contact with another body of water, her world spun. Lost in a confusing swirl of foam with lashings of water hitting her body in thousands of thuds, Lexa thrashed to keep her head above the surface. She took quick breaths each time her face broke free of the water, which bombarded her on every side. The everlasting roar of the waterfall rang in Lexa's ears.

Coughing and spluttering, Lexa finally found her bearings and swam away from the plunging waterfall. She looked up and spotted the huge castle looming over her. She grimaced, annoyed that the water betrayed her, leading her to the very last place she wanted to go.

But then, a dazzling light drew her attention. Small openings in the walls of the castle let out jets of water that fell to the bottom of the vast lake surrounding the castle.

A flicker of light piqued Lexa's curiosity, and she swam over to one of the small waterfalls.

Unable to get a good look at the light source, Lexa took a deep breath and ducked underwater again. Usually, she could hear the thoughts of fish and other creatures beneath the surface, like a constant chatter, but here there was nothing. Just an eerie silence that sent the hairs on the back of her neck on end.

Something was wrong.

The light grew stronger, and a gravitational pull beckoned Lexa to swim toward it. Discovering a narrow opening into the castle, she picked up her pace. Without hesitation, she squeezed through and stole enough courage to press forward, even though all her senses were on high alert.

She swam through a bed of dumbosies, glowing blue and lighting up the water as it often did when in contact with mermaid scales. When her lungs couldn't take a moment longer without oxygen, she poked her head up until her nose found fresh air and she inhaled deeply.

Looking around, she found herself in a hall with golden arches in the ceiling and blue light dancing along the stone walls. Flowers in full bloom shone like moonlight in shades of midnight blue. Lexa found the water's edge and pulled herself out, panting from all of the exertion. Her head pounded like a bell, and her stomach knotted.

She squeezed the skirt of her dress, then found her feet as she came to a shaky stand. The air was heavy and oddly still, and as Lexa breathed, she became acutely aware that she was the only source of any sound, which only intensified her alarm.

"What is this place?" she whispered to herself as she tiptoed around the hall. On the far side were what appeared to be a line of paintings, but as she drew closer to them, she held a hand over her mouth to stifle a gasp.

In swirls of dusty pink and navy blue were mermaids floating in water tanks, embedded in the stone walls. They hung like picture frames in some sort of twisted display.

If she had not been so horrified by the fact that these mermaids were being held captive, Lexa would have thought that they were beautiful. Like pieces of artwork.

A pair of sanguine eyes stared at her imploringly, and Lexa dashed toward the mermaid. She touched her palm up to the glass and opened her mouth to speak, but no sound came out. She was still mute.

What happened to you? Lexa asked telepathically.

The mermaid touched her slender hand to her throat and shook her head, a mass of blonde hair swooshing across her face.

Your voice is gone too? Lexa asked.

She nodded, then pressed her forehead to the glass. *My voice was stolen as soon as I began to sing. It happened to all of us here.*

Lexa clutched her throat, the flashback hitting her like an unexpected wave. She had been singing when her voice left her like a waltzing fog through the air, until she could no longer make a sound. And without her voice, she was almost powerless.

She turned back to the mermaid. *Who did this to you?*

The mermaid looked to Lexa's right and pointed to an iron door. Unsettled, Lexa looked at it and held her breath. But the urge to find answers was stronger than her sense of fear.

Whoever she was dealing with was ruthless and knew how to disarm a mermaid. But she needed to know for sure.

She marched to the iron door and pushed it open with a heavy squeak. The door swung forward, opening out to a huge hall. More mermaid tanks lined the walls, and the floor shimmered and sparkled like glitter. Lexa looked up to see the ceiling was made entirely of glass, and glowing blue water covered the ceiling from wall to wall.

To the far end was a raised platform with a collection of instruments and a large open space in the center of the hall. Lexa walked farther into the room, supposing this was where they had the mermaid auctions.

A sea of sad eyes followed her every move, and the eerie silence was only broken by her uneven breaths, along with the tapping of her feet hitting the stone floors as she crossed the room. Seeing so many mermaids floating in the tanks had her chest aching. Who was capable of such cruelty?

A young male mermaid caught her eye. He must have been in his late teens, with soft golden hair flowing around his broad shoulders. He looked stronger than the others, and his eyes shone like sapphires.

He looked familiar, but Lexa wasn't sure where she'd seen him before. Then it struck Lexa.

The water on the island had made her young again. What if it did the same thing to…?

Father! The thought-shrieked in her head. She hurried forward and clutched the glass in a desperate attempt to tear it apart and free her father from his cell.

What are you doing here? Don't tell me they took you too? Lexa's father said, pressing his head to the glass. Lexa shut her eyes and did the same as the two of them had a silent conversation.

When I learned of your disappearance, I had to find you.

Your mother appeared to me in what seemed like a dream. She told me you were in trouble, that you had been captured, but it was a trap. Pirates were waiting for me with spears made of elven metal. I couldn't move. They paralyzed me. Then I woke up in this place with Peter Pan taking my crown and using my trident to steal my voice. As he has done to the rest of our merpeople here.

Lexa's breath hitched as she listened to her father recount the events.

Long have we battled pirates who have been hunting our merpeople. But none have I found capable of this.

Lexa slammed her fist against the glass. *Daddy, I am so sorry. You are here because of me.*

Sweetheart, you need to go. Save yourself. Lead Atlantis. Be the queen I taught you to be.

I am not leaving without you.

There is no escaping this place. And the auction will take place in the morning. Without my trident, I am powerless. He raised his hands, revealing two brass shackles on both of his wrists. He didn't have to say it. Lexa knew they were made of elven metal. *You need to go before Pan finds out who you are.*

He already knows. Lexa touched her throat, and her father's brows furrowed.

He took your voice, too?

That's okay. I didn't come alone. I have friends helping me, and together, we will get you out of here.

There is no time. Not for you, anyway. Your legs won't last much longer. You must go.

Lexa frowned. *My legs are permanent, Father.*

Her father's eyes widened in concern. *Please, don't say so.*

Lexa's shoulder hunched in shame. *I made a deal with Neri.*

Lexa's father jumped back as though her words sent an electric current straight to his heart. Lexa blinked several times and looked at him apologetically as he rubbed his chest. *I had no choice.*

What deal did you make? Lexa's father looked at her legs briefly before shaking his head again.

Lexa hesitated, but only for a moment. *Neri will be Queen of Atlantis in the event that neither of us returns.*

He frowned. *Oh, Lexa. What have you done?*

Trust me, Father. I will return you to your throne. I just need to get your trident.

Before you go, I need you to promise me something, her father said, placing his hand on the glass. When Lexa hesitated, he gave her a stern look. *Promise me, Lexa.*

Lexa placed her palm against the glass over her father's hand. *Anything.*

No matter what happens to me, once you get your voice back, you will not sing the forbidden song.

Lexa's eyes widened. *But, Father—*

Promise. His thunderous tone shuddered in her mind. The forbidden song was rarely ever mentioned among mermaids. Lexa had only ever heard of one mermaid who had sung the words. It was to save the life of another, and she paid it with her own life. Life for a life. But it was forbidden because it opened the gates to the Underworld, which was ruled by a ruthless king named Hades.

Promise me, Lexa, her father demanded.

Lexa let out a defeated breath. *I promise.*

When she said nothing else, her father looked at her feet again. *How was Neri able to give you permanent legs without a trident?*

With this necklace. Here, I... Lexa touched the place where her necklace rested on her collarbone and frowned when she felt nothing there.

She gasped and looked wildly around her, wondering when her necklace had fallen off.

"Looking for this, I presume?"

Lexa jumped and swiveled on the spot to see Peter Pan standing in the open doorway, her necklace wrapped around his fist. The stone pendant dangled in the air.

Give that back, you thieving piece of scum! Lexa wanted to yell, but no sound came out. She clutched her neck, her throat burning as though she was spitting blades.

"Easy. You don't want to strain your vocal cords, now do you?" Peter said, giving her a wickedly lop-sided grin.

Lexa wanted nothing more than to punch that foolish smile off his face, but as she took a step forward, Peter raised his hand as though he was about to smash it on the floor.

Lexa froze, hardly daring to breathe as she watched him with panic. If he smashed the stone, she would lose her legs. And there would be nowhere else to go except into one of those tanks.

Her eyes moved from him to the pendant with a pleading look.

Peter cocked his head to the side, and his cheeks flushed with color like Lexa had told a marvelous joke. "I can't have you join my collection looking like that. What use is a mermaid with legs?"

Lexa stopped breathing as she watched Peter Pan swing his arm back. But just as he was about to thrust the stone to the ground, a shuffle of feet made him freeze in his tracks.

Wendy rushed in, her hands frantically moving, signing. Lexa could hardly keep up.

Peter! Please don't do this. It's me. Wendy Darling.

Peter blinked, his expression blank, but slowly he signed back. *Wendy?*

There was a stillness as the two of them merely looked at each other. Lexa dropped her hands and exhaled as she watched them for a silent moment.

Wendy stepped forward, her eyes glistening with tears. *Peter. It's me. Come back to me.*

Peter stayed frozen, but he blinked several times and his fingers twitched. *Wendy*…

He stared at Wendy like he was looking at a ghost. And maybe to him, she was. Who knew what had happened in their past.

Wendy took another step closer, and the air between them grew warm. Peter's face grew pink, and he shook his head, like he was clearing his mind.

Wendy. He held out his arms, his eyes brimming with tears. *My Wendy Darling.*

Wendy burst into tears and threw herself into his embrace. Lexa watched stunned as he held her tight. He patted her hair, squeezed her arms as she latched onto his neck.

Taking advantage of the moment, Lexa reached for her pendant and yanked it from Peter's grip. Startled, he turned to face her. She moved away from him, holding tight to her necklace. When Peter's eyes locked with Lexa, she was expecting to find a menacing stare, but instead, he watched her as if it was the first time he was seeing her.

He turned to Wendy, confused. *What happened? Where are we? Who is she?*

Wendy looked thoughtful for a moment, then turned to Lexa. *He was being hypnotized.*

Hypnotized? Peter repeated, looking at Wendy like she had sprouted two heads.

Lexa's head still throbbed with pain as she squinted at Peter, not knowing what to think. *Are you seriously telling me that you have no memory of kidnapping me? Or my father, for that matter?*

Peter frowned at Lexa, now looking at her like she was crazy. *What? No! Why would I do that? I don't even know who you are.*

Wendy paced the room, drumming her fingertips on her chin. Meanwhile, Peter raked a hand through his red hair and huffed.

You're not lying, Lexa said as she watched Peter, who had changed completely from the cold-hearted villain to a lost boy in a matter of moments. That also explained why he wasn't affected by her trance earlier.

But how was it that seeing Wendy just now broke him free from the hypnosis? And who would be using Peter Pan to run that twisted mermaid auction? And why would they have attacked Lexa and Ryke's crew?

Ryke!

Lexa turned to Wendy with a horrified expression. *Ryke! Where's Ryke?*

He's fine, Wendy assured her. *He was behind me. I just ran faster.*

We need to go find him. And get my father's trident. Lexa said, fastening her pendant around her neck, then turning to Peter. *Do you know who has Poseidon's trident?*

Peter answered the question with a mere glance at Wendy. No sign. No lip reading. Just a glance. And the answer had Wendy's eyes stretched wide.

Who? Lexa urged.

Wendy looked at Lexa, her expression pale and afraid. *Tinkerbell.*

CHAPTER FIFTEEN

RYKE

*B*y the time Ryke reached the steps of the dark castle, he was out of breath. He wondered how Wendy could have run so much faster than him. His chest burned with each ragged breath as he tried to keep up.

He halted at the sound of approaching footsteps from the top of the stairs. He strained his eyes in the darkness, looking for the outline of a person.

Who was it? A man… woman… fairy? The moonlight was too faint for him to distinguish any shapes. As the footsteps grew louder, he hid behind an alligator statue and pressed his back against the rough ridges of stone. He tightened his grip on the hilt of his sword and held his breath.

As the dark figure reached the statue, Ryke jumped out and drew his sword, pressing the tip of his blade against Peter Pan's back.

Peter raised his arms and stood still.

"Where's Lexa?" Ryke hissed.

A hand touched his shoulder, and Ryke swung around, brandishing his sword at whomever dared to come near. Lexa threw her palms up and hopped back so as not to get sliced by Ryke's steel blade.

"Lexa." Ryke sheathed his sword with an exhale, then moved toward her, scanning her from head to toe, making sure she was not hurt. Her cotton dress was damp and clung to her form like a second skin. He eyed the smears of dirt staining the pretty dress, and—to his utmost relief—he saw no blood. "Did he harm you?"

Lexa threw her arms around Ryke's neck. For a moment, his body flooded with heat, and he wanted to scoop her up and never let go, but she hadn't spoken a word, and the silence sent the hairs on the back of his neck on end.

"What did he do to you?" Ryke asked, pressing her protectively against him as though the act alone could stop anything bad from happening to her again.

"She can't speak," Peter said from behind Ryke. "Her voice is gone."

With Lexa still in his arms, Ryke turned to Peter with a deadly glare. "What do you mean, *gone?*"

When he didn't answer, Ryke ripped himself from Lexa and charged toward Peter. He grabbed him by his cotton shirt and pinned him to an olive tree. "What did you do to her voice?"

The curve of Ryke's hook pressed against Peter's face, and he threw his hands up in surrender. "It wasn't me," Peter said, his voice careful. "I was being mind-controlled."

"And you expect me to believe that?" Ryke snarled. He leaned in so close, the hot vapor of Peter's breath burned his cheeks.

Lexa reached for Ryke's hook and carefully moved it away from Peter's face. He looked at her, confused.

"He's telling the truth?" Ryke asked.

Lexa nodded, her eyes reflecting the moonlight. Ryke's eyes softened as he met Lexa's gaze. Then she began to sign.

"She's saying we have to find Tinkerbell,"

Peter said, only to get another angry glare from Ryke. "Tinkerbell is the one who had me mind-controlled. She's also the one who took Lexa's voice."

As much as Ryke wanted to pierce Peter in the gut, if he could communicate with Lexa and Wendy, he had no choice but to bring him along.

Lexa tugged on Ryke's arm. He shoved Peter toward a dirt path. Wendy hurried to his side with concern in her eyes.

"If you cross us in any way, you're dead," Ryke warned.

Peter signed to Wendy. If Ryke had to guess, he was probably telling her not to worry. But that wasn't true. Ryke would be watching his every move, and if Peter so much as stepped out of line, he was done.

Lexa rested her hand on Ryke's tense shoulder, and her touch soothed his irritation. He turned and brushed his thumb against her soft cheek. "We will find your voice again. I promise."

"This way," Peter called out ahead of them with Wendy by his side.

Ryke pressed his lips to Lexa's forehead before following Peter into the forest.

While Peter slashed his sword through the tangled foliage, forging a clear path for them, Ryke squeezed Lexa's hand, not wanting to ever let her go.

They came to a creek running up to a waterfall. The smell of wet grass flooded Ryke's nostrils. Wendy pointed into the foaming water, and Peter went to join her at the edge of the creek. Though it was night, the water let off a soft light of its own.

Peter crouched and picked up a glowing blue flower that floated on the water.

"What is that?" Ryke asked, curious at the sight. He had seen many strange and unexplainable things in his lifetime, but flowers glowing in the water was new for him.

Peter held it up. "It's dumbosie, but I'm not sure why it's glowing."

Lexa reached out, and Peter placed the flower on Lexa's palms. She stared at it for a moment. The soft light intensified the green in her eyes.

"What is it?" Ryke asked.

Lexa looked up and signed to Peter.

"It glows when it comes in contact with mermaid scales," Peter interpreted. "But it's also dangerous."

"What makes it dangerous?" Ryke pressed.

Lexa held up the flower as she signed. "This flower, when it glows, harnesses a hallucinogen element, which is the same hypnotic effect mermaids have when they sing."

Peter's eyes widened. "Like mind control?"

Lexa nodded.

Wendy gasped, then pointed to the distance. A tiny sparkle like that of a firefly swooped in the air toward them.

"Tinkerbell," Peter murmured venomously.

Wendy grabbed Peter by the arm and pulled him toward the darkness of the forest. Ryke did the same with Lexa, and they crouched behind a thick tree trunk. In silence, they watched as Tinkerbell flew down and picked up a dumbosie in her tiny hands and lifted it out of the water. Her arms strained as she carried the wet flower. It was three times bigger than her, so she ripped off a petal in the air and flew away with it.

Peter ran to the edge of the water with his hands balled into fists as he watched her fly away. And for the first time, Ryke believed him.

Wendy went to stand next to him and put a comforting hand on his shoulder. But his fists stayed clenched. Ryke couldn't blame him. The thought of being manipulated into burning someone alive wasn't something Ryke would let easily go either.

"She'll pay for what she did to me," Peter hissed, more for himself than anyone else.

Lexa touched Ryke's face, and the tips of her fingers brushed his stubble. The faint moonlight illuminated her face. She had dark rings under her eyes, and a sheen of sweat across her dainty brow, but her big shiny eyes blinked at him in the most tantalizing way. He picked up a lock of her hair, smooth as silk, and smiled. She was still as beautiful as he'd ever seen.

She brushed her finger over his chin, and it burned. He winced with a hiss, and she pulled away to reveal a bloodstain on her skin.

Her brows furrowed, and he took her hand and brought it down to his side, where he inter-twined his fingers with hers. "It's just a scratch," he assured her. "I'm okay." He caressed her face and brushed his thumb against her soft cheek. "I wish you could tell me how you're feeling."

She grabbed his hand and brought it to her

chest. Her heartbeat was so fast, he could feel it against his palm.

"Are you scared?"

She shook her head.

"Tired?"

She shook her head again, then placed her own hand over Ryke's heart. When her eyes met his, her gaze was so soft, and a warmth spread through his body. That was when Ryke understood what she was trying to tell him.

"You love me?"

A smile spread across her face, and she nodded.

His hand slid to the nape of her neck and pressed his lips to hers. The touch was soft, like velvet, and she tasted sweet as nectar. When her tongue found his, his mind spun on its axis. He wrapped his other arm around her waist, careful to avoid cutting her with his hook, and pulled her body up against him.

"I love you, too," he spoke against her lips, and though nothing else was said, so much was implied.

He was going to get her off that island, and as soon as he did, he was going to marry her and not wait a moment longer. He couldn't see a future any other way. Not any worth living without her.

He knew that he was irrevocably and hopelessly in love with her, and whatever happened next, Lexa's safety was all that mattered.

A melody from Peter's flute filled the air, and Ryke pulled back, turning toward the sound. A second later, the wild boys came into view with their weapons in hand. They stopped by the water's edge across the creek, and Ryke rose to his feet. He stepped in front of Lexa and put a protective arm in front of her. But before he could draw his sword, Peter raised a hand.

"It's okay," he said. "They're with me."

Ryke wrapped his fingers around his sword's hilt but didn't pull it out.

Peter signaled to them, and they dropped their weapons. Ryke relaxed his grip on the sword. Peter grabbed Wendy's hand and turned to Ryke.

"We're going to need them if we want to catch Tinkerbell," Peter said, pointing up to a tall tree in the distance. "She lives up there."

Ryke followed Peter's gaze and spotted something gold glowing at the top of the tree. Had it been moving it would have resembled a shooting star. But it wasn't. It was more still than the bright moon above them.

"What is that?" Ryke asked.

"Poseidon's trident," Peter said. "We need to get that back to him so he can free the mermaids. And return their voices."

Ryke didn't trust the wild boys tagging along. They were savages. But what other option did he have? He glanced at Lexa. If that was the only way to return her voice, he had no choice but to trust Peter and his wild friends.

He turned toward Peter, his hand still resting on the hilt of his sword. "So, how do we get up there?"

Peter squeezed Wendy's hand. "We stick together."

*A*s they stepped into a clearing, the wind blew, and the familiar smell of lilies filled the air. The image of Ryke's little sister surfaced in his mind, her golden locks bouncing joyfully over her shoulders as she picked flowers from the garden. As a nomad, Ryke rarely ever missed people or places. His sister was the only ache he ever felt of missing home. And the island after Lexa left. That was how he knew he was in love with her.

Ryke grabbed Lexa's hand and gave it a small squeeze. The light of the moon lit up her smile. As he debated pulling her in to steal a kiss, he bumped into the back of one of the wild boys, who grunted.

"Shh…" Peter brought a finger to his lips and looked around. Ryke scanned the clearing for any sign of danger, but there was none. The night was dark and silent, and only the buzzing of a firefly was heard above them.

After a few seconds, Peter signaled for the wild boys to keep moving. Ryke trailed behind them with Lexa at his side. As they pushed forward, the firefly that was above them flew ahead and began to hover over the lilies, flipping and turning as if it were dancing. It was a truly captivating sight, even from a distance.

Lexa stopped and squeezed Ryke's hand. He glanced at her and noticed her moonlit expression was tense. His legs froze in place as his body flooded with a sense of foreboding.

Lexa's wide eyes turned to Ryke, and he could

tell that if she could scream, she would. When his eyes found the firefly again, he finally understood what Lexa was trying to say.

"Tinkerbell!" Ryke yelled.

Her glittering wings swooped down toward the wild boys. They scattered. Tinkerbell flew into the lilies, hitting them with her wings like batting dust off a rug. Glittering yellow powder puffed from them like pollen, and suddenly, the wild boys broke into coughing fits.

"Run!" Peter yelled, turning on his heels and darting back toward Ryke and Lexa.

In one quick move, Lexa ripped a piece of fabric from her white cotton dress and pressed it to Ryke's nose and mouth. Though he had no idea what was happening, he held it in place as he followed Peter.

"Don't breathe in her pixie dust!" Peter called out breathlessly as they ran back through the dark woods.

"It's what she uses for mind control!"

Ryke stole a glance over his shoulder, and the glittering gold pixie dust danced in the air like a ghost with arms outstretched, ready to capture them.

He pushed his legs harder, but he was running

out of air. Recognizing that he was slowing down, Ryke knew he wasn't going to be able to outrun it.

"The waterfall!" he yelled, turning a sharp right while keeping Lexa at his side. He could hear Peter and Wendy following close behind. Then the sound of the plunging waterfall grew as strong as the smell of damp wood. "Jump!"

The four of them leaped in the air, leaving the pixie dust to scatter above them.

They splashed into the frigid water. Ryke waited until the yellow glow vanished before swimming back to the surface. Lexa punched the surface of the water with a grunt as she looked to the top of the waterfall. They had climbed for hours, and for what? Just to jump back down?

Tinkerbell flew away, then the wild boys' hunting call echoed in the distance.

"We have to go. We can't let them catch us," Peter said, swimming to the edge. "They're being controlled by Tinkerbell now. There's no telling what she's capable of. You saw what she had me do to your sailor."

"Why is she doing this?" Ryke asked, climbing out of the water and turning around to help Lexa. "What does she have against mermaids?"

"Other than using their dumbosie flower to

enhance her pixie dust, I have no idea," Peter said.

Wendy got to her feet and signed to him. "Wendy thinks she's working for someone."

"But who——" Ryke's question was cut off by a sharp pain on his side. He grunted, then dropped to his knees. Ryke blinked several times as his brain scrambled to make sense of the sudden pain. That's when he saw it. An arrow buried in his side.

The hunting call of the wild boys grew louder, and Lexa leaned down to help Ryke to his feet. He grimaced as he touched the arrow. He couldn't see in the dark, but the thick liquid was warm against his fingers. He lifted his hand, and the smell of iron flooded his senses.

Lexa's wide eyes turned to Peter as she signed frantically.

"We need to get you back to the ship," Peter interpreted.

"No." Ryke turned Lexa to face him. "We need to get the trident and save your father."

Peter hissed, then fell to the ground as an arrow shot past him, grazing his skin. He clamped his hand over the cut on his arm. "We need to get to the ship, now!"

Peter rose to his feet, only to grunt and fall down again. An arrow pierced the back of his leg. He pushed Wendy away and signed for her to run.

Ryke grabbed Peter from the ground and threw him over his shoulder, biting back the pain. Lexa led the way through the dark woods with Wendy at her side.

Ryke followed her lead, trying to ignore how every bone in his body ached. The sharp pain at his side began to burn and throb, and he winced with every step.

The sea air slapped his cheeks as they arrived back at the beach. Ryke spotted the ship bobbing in the distance, but the boat was gone. Ryke carefully laid Peter on the rocky sand, then dropped to his knees.

Lexa rushed to his aid and curled her fingers around the arrow that was still pierced at his side.

"Don't." He touched the back of her hand, panting. "The arrow is stemming the blood flow. It'll be worse if you remove it."

She frowned, then swung his arm around her shoulder, helping him to his feet. But when she started toward the ocean, he stopped her.

"No," Ryke said through heavy breaths.

Lexa looked at him in confusion, the cold snap of the sea breeze tossed her hair back, and Ryke's heart ached to see her so concerned.

"Take Wendy," he said.

Lexa shook her head, but he brushed her cheek with the back of his finger. "Don't worry about me. Right now, I need you to be safe."

Lexa grabbed Ryke's face with both hands and pressed her lips to his. The sweetness of her lips gave him a shot of adrenaline, and all of his pain was gone for the time her lips remained on his. When she pulled back, her eyes said more than her words ever could. And in that moment, with nothing but the crashing waves next to them, he memorized every feature of her face, just in case he never saw her again.

Footsteps approached, and Ryke drew his sword. "Lexa, go!"

Lexa pulled Wendy away from Peter, then dove with her into the ocean. Once Ryke saw that Lexa was swimming away, he stepped in front of Peter, who was still on the ground with a bleeding leg.

"Stop hiding, you cowards!" he yelled, rage ripping through his throat. "Come out where I can see you!"

The wild boys came into view, stepping out from the dark forest, holding their makeshift weapons.

The pain on Ryke's side shot down his leg as he struggled to balance himself. But he held his ground, keeping the sword in front of him. There was no way he would win against them all, but he sure wasn't going down without a fight. And if he ever caught that firefly, he would squish her like a bug.

Peter touched Ryke's boot. "Don't hurt them," he begged. "They don't know what they're doing. They're under her control."

"How did you break out of her control?" Ryke asked.

"I saw Wendy," Peter said. "Maybe my memories of her broke me from the trance."

One of the wild boys lunged a spear, and Ryke swung his sword, splitting it in midair. "Then we better think of something quickly because they're not going to hold anything back."

Another spear came at them, and Ryke split it with his sword again.

Peter reached into his pocket and pulled out a wooden flute.

Ryke arched a brow. "You're going to play them a song?"

Peter shrugged. "Maybe they'll hear something that'll bring good memories." He brought it to his mouth and started to play. The joyful melody carried in the wind, and the scowl on each of their faces began to soften.

"I think it's working," Ryke said, surprised.

The wild boys shook their heads, then looked at one another, stunned and confused. But then an arrow pierced Peter's flute, bringing the music to a stop and splitting the wood in his hand.

The deadly stare returned to the eyes of the wild boys, and they raised their weapons once more.

Peter scrambled with the broken flute and tried blowing into it, but the sound it made was that of a screeching bird. It did nothing to the boys but rile them up even more.

Ryke's arm was growing tired. His sword had never been so heavy. His wound was throbbing.

Peter dragged himself backward to get away, but there was nowhere to go. With his bleeding calf, he wouldn't even be able to swim, let alone run. And Ryke, with an arrow still pierced at his side, wouldn't be able to swim either, let alone carry Peter with him.

Peter pushed himself up, grimacing.

"What are you doing?" Ryke asked, holding on to Peter's arm.

"They're my responsibility," Peter said, limping forward to stand in front of Ryke. "I'll hold them off. You go after Lexa."

Ryke pressed the curve of his hook against Peter's chest and stopped him from stepping in front of him. "I never leave men behind." He turned to face the wild boys and braced himself.

A loud gunshot released in the air. The wild boys swung around to find Ryke's crew aiming their guns in their direction. The boys howled their hunting call into the night sky, then dropped their weapons in the sand. Then, one by one, they began to shake their heads as they came out of the trance. They looked around in a haze, confused as to where they were and how they had gotten there.

Ryke dropped his hand with the heavy sword, then signaled to his crew. "Lower your weapons. They're no longer a threat."

"Always so trusting," a familiar voice came from a distance.

Ryke squinted into the darkness, recognizing the voice at once. "Uncle?"

The King of the Shores stepped onto the beach with his hands behind his back. His royal garment stretched out behind him. He didn't look young like Ryke and the rest of his crew. He must not have consumed the water from the island.

"Lock them all on the ship," the King ordered, and before long, all the wild boys were bound by their hands with ropes. Peter was taken on a wooden gurney back into the forest. Ryke guessed that the King's boat must've been on the other side of the island.

"How did you find this place?" Ryke asked.

The King strolled toward Ryke. "How about we remove that arrow from you and get you some clean clothes?"

Ryke's head began to spin, and he struggled to keep his balance. "Lexa is not going to marry the Prince. I will not allow it."

The King stopped in front of Ryke. He watched him for a long moment without a word, then before Ryke could stop him, he ripped the arrow out of Ryke's side. A sharp pain shot up Ryke's body like a lightning bolt. Ryke's brain twisted in his skull, and nausea rose from his stomach. The world around him became a blur of oceans and stars as his body hit the sand.

He could barely see his uncle towering over him.

Then everything went black.

CHAPTER SIXTEEN

LEXA

*L*exa fell with Wendy onto the wooden floor of the ship, drenched and panting. She looked around. They were alone on the ship, no crew, no captain.

Lexa pushed herself to her knees, then turned to Wendy. *I have to go back for Ryke.* But before she could rise to her feet, Wendy grabbed her arm.

It isn't safe.

All the more reason he needs me, Lexa said. *And I cannot leave my father.*

Then why did we swim to the ship? Wendy asked.

A cunning smile tugged at Lexa's lips. *Weapons.*

She jumped to her feet, ignoring her wobbly

legs, and rushed to the captain's quarters where she knew Ryke kept the swords and knives.

She handed a couple to Wendy, then sheathed two knives under her dress after holstering a sheath to her waist for a sword.

Wendy glanced at Lexa furtively. With each passing minute, Lexa's heart throbbed, and she couldn't catch a breath. She couldn't wait to return to Ryke's aid.

When Wendy gave her yet another teary-eyed look, Lexa grunted.

They're still alive, Wendy. She signed with trembling hands. *I know they are.*

No, she didn't. And as time went on, the likelihood of their survival diminished. But Lexa pushed the thought to the back of her mind and hurried to grab a sword.

Once the weapons were secured, they ran back to the upper deck. Lexa threw herself against the side and clutched the railing until her knuckles turned white as she squinted toward the beach. It was empty. Did the wild boys take them back into the forest? Were they getting ready to be hanged?

Wendy tugged on Lexa's dress, then pointed to the other side of the ship. Lexa followed her gaze, and her breath caught in her throat. Another ship bobbed in the distance.

Wendy began to sign at top speed. *Look at those cages hanging in the air. Aren't they Peter's wild boys? Do you think Peter is on the ship too?*

Lexa swallowed an uncomfortable lump in her throat. She could see the flag. The ship belonged to the King of the Shores. Ryke's uncle. Lexa held her breath, looking for any signs of Ryke. Surely, his uncle would have saved him? But Ryke was nowhere to be seen. A sudden movement caught her eye, and she squinted to get a better look.

It was Peter. He was tied up and gagged while being hoisted up on a gurney.

Wendy gasped next to Lexa.

A sickly sensation swirled in Lexa's stomach, and all of her senses screamed that something terrible was happening. And she could not see Ryke anywhere.

Her knees grew weak, and a flash of pain shot right through her chest as her mind came up with the thought that Ryke was dead.

As Lexa was about to climb up on the railing, Wendy touched her arm.

If you go to the ship, I'll return to the beach, Wendy said.

Why? Lexa asked.

Wendy's brows furrowed. *Someone needs to stop Tinkerbell.*

Lexa nodded. *Do what you must. Just be safe.* She then pulled Wendy into a hug.

Wendy darted across the other side of the ship toward the rope ladder while Lexa climbed up on the railing. She wasted no time jumping into the water. She swam as fast as she could, wishing she was in her mermaid form again. It would have been much easier with her fin. But she needed to get to Ryke. And she swam as hard as her body would allow until she reached the back of the ship.

Lexa's arms burned as she lifted herself up and snuck into the ship by pushing a canon and crawling in through an opening. She tiptoed along the lower deck and listened for the low murmuring of the men walking on the deck above her head.

Careful not to be seen, Lexa searched through the cabins. And just when any glimmer of hope was gone, she found the captain's quarters with its light on.

She opened the door and snuck in, closing it quietly behind her. She turned, and her eyes landed on a sleeping figure on a makeshift bed in the corner of the cabin. There he was, bundled up in blankets, with his jet-black hair drenched in sweat, clinging to his temples.

Ryke.

Lexa sank to her knees by the bed, and after removing her sword and placing it on the floor, she smoothed Ryke's hair from his clammy forehead. His eyes fluttered open with a wince, but then his eyes met hers, and he jerked forward with a grimace.

Lexa shushed him and planted her hands on his chest, feeling his firm pectorals through the cotton shirt. She wanted to tell him to rest, but her voice was still gone.

"You have no idea how happy I am to see your beautiful face," he murmured, bringing his hands to her cheek and grazing her with his thumb. The touch sent tingles through her body, and she lowered her head and kissed his salty lips. It was gentle and brief. Then she lifted his shirt to see that the arrow was gone, and in its place was a fresh bandage wrapped around his torso.

Lexa let out a deep sigh of relief and returned to meet Ryke's eyes. As much as she wanted to stay with him, she still needed to get her father's trident. And she needed to free him before the King did. Otherwise, she would have to abide by their agreement, and the mere thought of her marrying someone who wasn't Ryke made her heart throb in pain.

She caressed his face and peered into his deep blues, wishing that she had her voice so she could tell him just how much she loved him. And how much she needed him at her side. But he was in no condition to tag along, so as much as it pained her, she needed to go without him.

As if reading her thoughts, Ryke grabbed her arm and held her gaze. "I'm coming with you," he breathed. But he could barely keep his eyes open, let alone fight. Though, not even Lexa knew who she was going up against. Who really was Tinkerbell, and what did she gain by auctioning mermaids?

"We mustn't let my uncle save Poseidon," Ryke spoke as if he was having a nightmare. "You will not marry the Prince. I will not allow it. I will not bear it."

Lexa frowned and brushed the tip of her fingers over his stubble. His eyes fluttered open once more, and she held his gaze for a long moment. He must've sensed the farewell in her eyes, because he jolted forward and pressed his lips to hers with such desperation and passion, it took her breath away.

Ryke seemed unaware of his injuries as he roughly fisted her hair and pulled her into him to deepen the kiss. Lexa almost fell on his chest, and propped herself up as Ryke tasted her, his stubble dragging across her chin in the most delicious way. Lexa gasped against his mouth, and her eyes rolled back as the passion rose to dizzying heights. The two of them explored each other, until finally, Lexa ripped away to catch a breath.

Ryke leaned his forehead against hers as they both exhaled. "We will retrieve the trident and release your father before my uncle does," Ryke said, his voice sounding as beautiful as birdsong in the morning. He caressed her cheek, looking at her lips. "And once your father is safe, I will ask him for your hand in marriage."

Lexa leaned in to kiss him again, unable to stop smiling. And if she had her voice, she would scream a million times *yes*.

The door opened, and Lexa tore her lips from Ryke as she backed away, startled.

The King of the Shores strode in, his bushy brows rising briefly at the sight of her, but then his face broke into an amicable smile. "Finally, it all makes sense," he said, walking to his desk and picking up a glass. "I have been so puzzled as to why you have been dead set against this arranged marriage, Ryke, but now I see the real reason."

Ryke grimaced as he pushed himself to sit up. Lexa hurried to help him, and he grasped her hand. "We have done nothing wrong."

The King scowled. "Fooling around with the Prince's betrothed is punishable by death."

Lexa's eyes widened in horror, and she squeezed Ryke's hand. Ryke rose to his feet, wincing and struggling to keep his balance, then stepped protectively in front of Lexa. "She is not betrothed to the Prince. And she never will be."

Prince Tristan walked in and looked from Ryke to Lexa, then back to Ryke again. Finally, he turned his attention to his father, who was taking a greedy gulp of his strong drink. "What is the matter?"

He looked back, and his gaze lowered to Lexa's hand, still holding Ryke's. Lexa wanted to say something, anything, but there was no need. The Prince got the message.

"The wedding is off," he said, turning to his father again.

"You say that as if you have a choice," the King said firmly.

Lexa frowned and glanced at Ryke, but the Prince cleared his throat. "No. I will not stand in the way of my cousin's happiness." He crossed his arms across his royal uniform, and for the first time, Lexa saw the Prince Wendy had praised him to be.

The King met his stare for several moments while Lexa exchanged looks with Ryke. She could see in his eyes that they were both waiting with bated breath.

The King picked up a small pouch from the inside of his coat, then turned to Ryke with darkened eyes. "We'll see about that." His arm swooped like an arch, and a cloud of yellow pixie dust filled the air. The Prince leaped forward. Lexa hitched a breath, thinking that the Prince was going to hurt Ryke, but then the golden powder covered the Prince's head. He coughed and blinked while Ryke covered his nose and mouth with his shirt.

Lexa's mind grappled with her thoughts, trying to find any plausible reason for the King to have used pixie dust, but nothing added up.

"Guards," the King called, his nostrils flaring

as he looked at his disoriented son. Lexa thought she saw a hint of disappointment on his face, but it faded and turned serious.

Two burly men shouldered their way into the small cabin, their boots thudding the wood so hard their footsteps were like drum beats.

"Take the Princess to her quarters," the King ordered. Then he turned to his son and muttered two words that sent an icy current down her spine. "Kill Ryke."

Lexa wanted to scream, but no sound came out as she opened her mouth. One guard pinned Ryke to the wall while the other grabbed Lexa by the arms and yanked her toward the door. She wrestled against him, but it was no use as the guard carried her out of the room.

"Let her go!" Ryke demanded, but as they rounded the corner, she could no longer see him.

Ryke's voice grew faint as he tried reasoning with his cousin. Hot tears leaked out of Lexa's eyes as she was carried through the narrow halls. She grimaced at the searing pain in her chest. It was as if the King had rammed a hot poker stick right through her heart.

"Here you are, Princess." They came to a filthy cell, which was empty except for a rotten bucket sitting in the corner. Only a peep of moon-light streamed in through one of the holes resem-bling a window. The guard pushed Lexa inside, and with a jarring squeak, the door locked shut. Lexa stumbled to find her balance, then swiveled on the spot, scowling at the guards.

They chuckled to each other at some unspoken joke and marched off. Lexa chewed her lip, her eyes darting all around as she took in her surroundings. The cells are designed for animal stock, not prisoners. There must have been a weakness somewhere.

Just then, Lexa heard the most beautiful sound. The squawk of a seagull nearby.

She ran to the small opening in the ship and pressed her face to it.

I heard the guards talking. They've taken her here. Hurry up, Bob!

It was Hackett, and Lexa's heart leaped at the sound of his voice in her mind.

I'm here! Lexa cried out in her mind.

A scuttling sound flew up the side of the ship, and the welcome sight of a little red lobster appeared before her. *Lexa, I am mighty relieved to see you alive.*

Their joyful reunion was short-lived when the

foreboding beats of a drum interrupted them. *I'm alive, yes. But if we don't move fast, the same can't be said for Ryke.*

Hackett squawked again, and Lexa heard him swoop up into the sky. Meanwhile, Bob scurried inside the cell.

Well? Can't you do something? Lexa asked him. His beady eyes looked startled.

What do you think I am? I can't exactly pick a lock with these! He raised his pincers and snapped them furiously. Lexa reached for a knife she had taken from Ryke's quarters and showed it to Bob.

Will this work?

The drumbeats were steady as Lexa watched Bob trying to pick the lock. *What is that sound?* she asked.

Someone is walking the plank, Hackett replied as he soared outside the window.

A lump formed in Lexa's throat. They were running out of time. Not only were Peter and the wild boys going to walk the plank into crocodile-infested waters, but…

Lexa frowned as she looked at Bob. *They're going to kill Ryke.*

CHAPTER SEVENTEEN

RYKE

*R*yke shoved the guard off of him, then turned to the Prince, who dismissed the guard at once.

"I'll deal with him," he said with a menacing glare.

Ryke lifted his hook defensively in front of him. "Cousin, you don't want to do this."

"*Cousin?*" The Prince snorted. "You abandon your family and live as a nomad for years, and now you dare call me *cousin?*"

"We are family—"

"No, we're not." The Prince pulled out a knife from his sheath and glared at Ryke. "You are nothing but a despicable pirate trying to steal my throne."

"Your throne?" Ryke stared at his cousin in disbelief. "What on the blazing stars has that pixie dust done to you? I have never desired the throne. You know that."

"Why else would you want to marry that fish?"

"Watch it!" Ryke puffed out his chest. "That is the woman I love. Don't you dare speak of her in that manner."

The Prince chuckled. "Don't worry... *cousin*. By the time I'm done with you, I'll make sure she's never spoken of again."

"This isn't you," Ryke barked, but winced as his thunderous voice reverberated through his injured body. He could feel his strength fading. He raised his arms. "Listen to me, you are being mind-controlled."

The Prince's eyes were blank, and Ryke wondered what it would take to break the trance. He needed to find Peter. He had broken free once before. Something about seeing Wendy.

"I heard enough from you." The Prince tossed his knife in the air only to catch it again with the sharp blade facing down. "I'll tell Lily you said goodbye."

At hearing his sister's name, Ryke charged

toward his cousin, pinning his knife-hand against the wall. But Tristan's free hand balled into a fist and struck Ryke in his wounded side. A sharp pain shot through Ryke's body like a jolt of electricity. He stumbled backward with his head spinning, but before the Prince could strike him again, Ryke ran out of the captain's quarters, staggering down the narrow hallway.

"Ryke!" His cousin barked, stomping behind him. "Get back here!"

Ryke pushed his legs harder, and it felt like needles covered his entire body. But he needed to get to the upper deck. He needed to find Peter. It was the only way to save his cousin. And himself.

"Ryke!" Tristan's angry voice was much closer than before, and it took all of Ryke's strength to hurry up the stairs. As soon as he reached the top, he fell to the ground, panting and aching. A guard hurried to his aid, and in one quick swoop, Ryke snatched his sword.

The guard stepped back as Ryke's blade pressed to the man's chest. "Where is Peter Pan?" he asked through clenched teeth.

"In bonds," the guard said, pointing to the front of the ship. "He's about to walk the plank."

Ryke limped to the front of the ship until he

spotted Peter sitting inside a wooden cage with his head down. Ryke snuck from behind and poked Peter's leg with his sword.

Peter looked up.

Before he could say anything, Ryke shushed him, then waved him to come closer. Peter jumped to his feet and pressed his face against the wooden bars. "What is the meaning of this? I have done nothing wrong."

"I know," Ryke agreed, keeping his voice low. "They are after me too."

"Why?"

"Because of Lexa."

Peter's brows furrowed. "I already told you, I was in a trance. I would never have taken the Princess otherwise."

"Tell me about this trance," Ryke pressed. "How did you break free from it?"

"Ryke!" Tristan's voice was distant, but it was only a matter of time before he was close enough to stab Ryke. And even though he would put up a fight, he was too injured to win. "You can hide, but you can't run!"

Ryke grunted under his breath, then scowled at Peter. "If you don't tell me how you broke free from that blazing trance, we are both going to die."

Peter's eyes widened, and Ryke was fairly certain that he wasn't worried about the crocodiles as much as the mermaids. Who knew what Tinkerbell had him do to them on that island.

Peter reached through the wooden bars and grabbed Ryke's shirt. "I can't be thrown in there! They'll drown me at once!"

"Then tell me how to break the blasted trance!"

"I don't know!" Peter shook his head furiously, his hands trembling as he clung to Ryke's shirt. "Where's Wendy?"

Ryke sheathed his sword, then grabbed Peter's hand. "Calm down. I need you to focus."

"Wendy," Peter said in a shaky, panicked tone. "Wendy—"

Ryke reached inside the cage and grabbed Peter by the back of the neck, then pressed his pale face between the wooden bars. He kept him pinned there until their eyes locked. "Focus, Peter."

"I don't know. It was Wendy," Peter said. "She broke the trance. She freed me."

Before he could say anything else, a sudden

memory surfaced in Ryke's mind. Many years ago, a siren's song had overtaken his senses. He was sixteen and he'd been strolling on the beach. The song drew him into the water, then pulled him into the deep like an anchor hitting the ocean floor. He flowed in a heavenly bliss until he could no longer breathe. But panic never set in because the angels were singing.

Then he heard his sister's cries. It was faint and distant from above the water, but the high-pitched sound broke through the haze as she cried out his name. She needed him. He was the only family she had left after their parents died, and she needed him. That thought snapped him back at once.

Ryke loosened his grip on Peter's neck, then stepped back. "Love…" he murmured. "Love will bring him back."

"Bring who back?" Peter asked.

"There you are." The Prince appeared on the other side of the cage with blood dripping from his knife.

Ryke's eyes widened, and he jumped out from behind the cage, drawing his sword and holding his side. "Where's Lexa?"

"She's locked away," the Prince replied, a

wicked grin growing on his face. "Just like her *father*."

Ryke's hand dropped as he stared at the Prince's blank eyes again. "You're not my cousin."

His wicked grin grew wider. "Aren't you an observant little one?"

"It's Tinkerbell!" Peter yelled, yanking at the wooden bars. "Guards, seize him! He's being controlled by a ruthless fairy!"

But there were no guards around. That imposter must've sent the guards elsewhere.

Ryke cocked his head, watching his cousin as he moved from side to side, swirling the bloody knife in his hand.

"I have heard many stories about you," the imposter said. "And I must confess, I am impressed. Not many pirates survive to tell tales of the sea. You most certainly are the most fearless pirate I have ever met." The Prince bowed his head. "It will be an honor killing you."

Ryke narrowed his eyes, trying to see through his cousin. A fairy wouldn't know the tales of the sea. And she most certainly would not have met pirates because they knew better than to come near Neverland.

No, the imposter wasn't Tinkerbell.

Ryke gripped his sword and raised it in front of him again. "I know who you are," he said, replaying the words his cousin had said just moments earlier when Ryke had asked about Lexa.

"She's locked away… just like her father."

Had there not been so much disdain in the word *father*, Ryke wouldn't have guessed it. But there was only one person who, according to Lexa, hated Poseidon more than anyone.

"Neri," Ryke hissed.

Another wicked smile spread across the Prince's face. "And here I was having so much fun blaming it on Tinkerbell."

Peter's mouth fell open, and he backed away from the bars.

"Let my cousin go," Ryke demanded. "Fight me in your own skin."

Neri chuckled. "You can't even fight your human Prince. What makes you think you can win against the Queen of the Sea?"

"You're not the queen. It's Lexa's throne, not yours," Ryke said, watching as the imposter's amused expression was replaced by a glare. That was when Ryke knew he'd struck a nerve.

"You've just spoken your last words, *pirate*," Neri hissed venomously, like a dethroned queen.

Ryke braced himself for the blow he knew would follow, but instead, his cousin stepped back and raised the bloody knife to the heavens. The winds picked up from a light breeze to a violent howl. Thunder rumbled in the distance as lightning cracked the black sky.

A sudden flash of lightning struck Ryke's sword, sending him flying across the ship. His back hit a wooden beam, then he fell on the floor. Pain shot up his arm and sizzled through his body. His head spun, and ears rang. The floor beneath him moved, and nausea rose from the pit of his stomach.

A heavy boot pinned him down, and he shot his eyes open. The imposter towered over him, holding a sword to his throat.

"I told you that you didn't have what it takes to go against the Queen of the Sea."

Ryke grimaced as the boot pressed at his wound. And when the imposter raised the sword with both hands, ready to pierce Ryke through the chest, he closed his eyes and thought about Lexa. And what he wanted his final words to be.

"I love you, Lexa."

The clang of metal against metal rang loudly in his ear. He shot his eyes open only to find Lexa on her knees next to him, blocking Neri's fatal strike with a sword.

When their eyes locked, there was a glimmer of playfulness in them, as if she were saying, *I love you, too.* He chuckled, and she smiled. Then without another thought, she swung her sword around until it slipped from Neri's grip and was flung overboard.

His chest puffed with pride as he watched her rise to her feet, sword in hand. Neri stepped back, swirling the bloody knife again.

Ryke waited to hear the venomous words that were clearly on the tip of her tongue, but nothing came out. Neri and Lexa simply stared at each other in silence for a long time.

That was when Ryke realized they were communicating telepathically.

"Lexa!" Peter's voice came from somewhere on the ship. Before long, he joined Lexa with a sword of his own.

Lexa crouched next to Ryke and swung one of his arms around her shoulder to help him to his feet. He grimaced as the wound on his side stretched open. As he touched it, the warm liquid spread across the bandage. He didn't have to look at it to know he was bleeding.

"Thanks for that lightning, by the way," Peter said to the imposter in a smug tone. "You released us all."

The wild boys suddenly stepped into view, holding broken pieces of wood as weapons.

"Guards!" the Prince barked. "Seize them!"

Heavy footsteps rushed toward them at the back of the ship, and Peter howled a battle cry. The wild boys howled in return, then turned their attention to the wave of guards that came at them.

Lexa's veins seemed to pump with adrenaline as she tied her long hair back and ran to fight alongside the wild boys. She dashed forward, throwing her sword this way and that. Sometimes, it met with a clash of steel, other times, the blade met with flesh, accompanied by a grimace. Lexa shoved a guard so hard that he almost fell overboard. As he struggled to find his feet, Lexa hopped over him and kicked him over.

She picked up the guard's fallen sword and tossed it to Ryke. He caught it midair with a wince. Another guard came at her. She ducked and blocked the attacks, then kicked the guard on the stomach. He crashed against a stack of wooden crates and fell in a heap on the ground.

A bird cocked from above them, and Lexa swung around. When she gasped, Ryke turned to see.

Tinkerbell was carrying Poseidon's trident above the trees. A swirl of pixie dust danced around them as they glided toward the ocean.

Ryke gasped at the realization that Tinkerbell was taking the trident to Neri.

"No!" he yelled, feeling every muscle in his injured body ache.

Lexa placed two fingers between her lips and blew a loud whistle. Hackett cocked in reply, then darted toward Tinkerbell. Lexa picked up Bob from the floor, then ran to the front of the ship. A frightened sound ripped from the lobster's throat as Lexa hurled him in the air.

He grabbed the trident with his claws and ripped it from Tinkerbell's grip. He soared in the air for a long moment, then began to fall toward the sea.

More lightning cracked the sky, and Ryke spotted Neri in the distance. A frightening screech ripped through the lobster's throat as he hurled down toward the monstrous tentacles thrashing in the waters below.

But then Hackett swooped down and grabbed Bob, along with the trident, just before one of Neri's tentacles took hold.

Lexa leaped with joy at the front of the ship as she watched Hackett fly away with her father's trident back toward Neverland. If Ryke had to guess, Lexa must've told Hackett telepathically where to find her father, and before long, Poseidon would once again hold power over his kingdom.

A bubble of pride rose inside Ryke as he watched Lexa still jumping for joy. But then he caught a movement to his left and spotted his cousin running farther to the back of the ship.

Ryke limped after him with a sword in hand. Though it was too heavy for him to lift it up. "It's over. You lose."

Neri had Tristan stop by a stack of wooden crates, then turn around slowly. "I guess you're right," he said in a low tone. "It is over."

He raised the bloody knife in the air, but it wasn't until the moonlight reflected on the blade that Ryke realized who was its next target.

"No!" Ryke dropped the sword and charged

toward his cousin. He swerved the knife with his hook, aiming it away from Tristan's heart. He fell on top of him and pinned him down. The knife slid across the wooden floor until it splashed into a thick liquid only a few feet away.

Ryke blinked several times, willing his eyes to focus and his sight to sharpen. A woman in a dark cloak rested on her knees next to a body that laid in a pool of its own blood. Her blonde hair seeped out of the hood of her cloak as she stared down at her hands. They were covered in blood.

"Father?" Tristan choked out, his body trembling beneath Ryke.

"Cousin?"

The Prince looked up at Ryke, his eyes back to their original blue. "Ryke?" He gave his cousin a puzzled look. "What happened?"

Ryke rolled off of his cousin, and the Prince crawled toward the bleeding corpse. "Father?" He scooped up the body and cradled him in his arms. When his head fell back, Ryke could see his uncle's lifeless eyes wide open. "No! Father, no!"

The woman in the dark cloak rose to her feet, then backed away slowly as if in shock. But Ryke couldn't see her face. It was too dark.

"You!" Tristan turned toward her with a deadly glare. "You killed the King!"

When she swung around, the Prince grabbed her cloak. He yanked it off her, revealing her long, blonde curls.

"Guards!" the Prince barked, his voice trembling. "She killed the King! Seize her!"

A wave of footsteps came rushing toward them, and the woman began fidgeting in every direction. She was clearly in a panic. Ryke couldn't blame her. Killing the King was punishable by death.

The Prince tossed her cloak aside, then rose to his feet. "Stop!" he yelled at the woman.

She swung around, but her face was cast in shadow from the stacked crates.

"Whoever you are," the Prince spoke through clenched teeth, "surrender at once."

The woman jumped up on the railing, and without any hesitation, dove into the ocean. Tristan ran toward the railing and reached out to grab her. The tips of his fingers brushed against her clothes, then a second later, she splashed in the water.

"Get me a boat, now!" the Prince ordered, squinting into the dark waters. "Guard!"

Ryke pushed himself up, grimacing with every breath, then limped toward his uncle. He crouched next to his lifeless body and closed his uncle's eyes.

May your kingdom have peace now that you're gone.

He picked up the cloak from the floor and covered his uncle with it. He stared at the cloth for a moment, feeling a deep ache in his heart.

And may you have peace wherever you go.

"Ryke!" Lexa's voice was back, and the sweet melody made his heart soar. He pushed himself to his feet and limped toward the sound.

"Lexa!" he called back. As he rounded the corner, he spotted her running toward him.

"Ryke!" She leaped into his arms, and he bit back the pain that rippled through his body. "My voice is back!"

And it was the sweetest sound he'd ever heard. But most importantly, it meant that her father was safe. And they could finally be together for the rest of their lives. So long as they kept her necklace safe, she would have legs, and she could stay with him. He nuzzled her hair, the salty smell of the ocean filling his senses.

"Oh, my love, we did it!" She pulled back, beaming. "We did it."

Ryke brushed his thumb over her porcelain cheek. He couldn't wait to make her his wife and caress her entire body with the same tenderness. "Yes, we did, my love." He closed his eyes and leaned in, eager to taste her sweet lips.

But she was suddenly ripped from his arms, and he shot his eyes open.

Lexa was on the floor of the ship with a large black tentacle wrapped around her leg, screaming as the tentacle dragged her toward an opening on the side of the ship. Ryke jumped toward her and grabbed her arms. They were dragged together until Peter and the wild boys grabbed Ryke by the shirt and pulled him back. Lexa's arms slid off of Ryke's, and he lost his grip on her.

"No!" he screamed as he watched her slide off the side of the ship, then splash into the dark waters. "Lexa!"

Ryke pushed Peter off of him and ran to the edge. He peered into the water, but it was too dark. He climbed on the railing, but before he could jump, Peter tackled him to the floor. "That's a bad idea!"

"Get off of me!" Ryke demanded.

"You can't possibly think you can fight against a sea monster in the water and still survive!"

"She's going to drown!" Ryke's throat burned as the words came out. He shoved Peter aside and staggered to his feet.

"She's a mermaid. How could she drown?" Peter asked.

"As long as she has legs, she can't breathe underwater," Ryke said, turning toward the spot where he'd last seen Lexa. "I may not be able to beat that sea monster, but you can bet the blazing stars, I will not let Lexa die."

And without another word, he jumped in after her.

CHAPTER EIGHTEEN

LEXA

*L*exa held her breath, but from the iron grip Neri's tentacle had on her leg, cutting off blood supply and giving her pins and needles in her foot, to the rush of water flowing through her hair, she knew soon her lungs would give out. The salty seawater that used to bring comfort now stung her eyes. And as Neri brought Lexa deeper, the fading moonlight filled Lexa's heart with dread.

She clutched her necklace and shut her eyes as thoughts spiraled like a cyclone in her mind. Neri's cruel laugh flooded the space around her. Then panicked cries surrounded them as they shot like a cannonball deeper and deeper into the darkness, and Lexa could just make out a silver fin above her.

Her chest grew stiff as seconds stretched into long minutes. Lexa needed oxygen. And at that moment, there was only one way to get it. But in doing so, she'd be breaking her own heart.

She reached for her pedant, but before she could even think to shatter it, Neri stopped dragging her and another tentacle wrapped around Lexa's torso and arms.

Now, now, not so fast. Neri's bright purple eyes dazzled Lexa as they beamed at her like two jewels near a flame. The purple dots grew bigger as her smile widened, and for a second, Lexa wondered how Neri was going to kill her. Would she pierce a tentacle straight through her heart, or simply let her drown?

Her lungs ached, and it was as if her organs were constricting inside her body.

Neri ripped Lexa's necklace from her and held the pendant in her broad hand. Lexa tried reaching for it, but her lungs were on fire and she was growing weaker by the second. As much as it pained Lexa to lose a future with Ryke, crushing the pendant was her only chance at survival.

Neri's smile turned devilish, and she tightened her grip around Lexa's body, squeezing the last of her breath out of her. Lexa held on, but she could feel her mind fading to black as her eyes rolled back.

But then Neri flinched, and her grip loosened for a fraction of a second. Bewildered, Lexa forced her eyes open to see a rush of bubbles surrounding her like a cyclone. Only this one brought the most beautiful sight, which made her wonder if she was dreaming.

Jinko soared through the water with Ryke clinging on to his fin. He grabbed Lexa and held on as Jinko rushed to the surface. Once her face hit the open air, Lexa took greedy gulps of air. She held onto Ryke, and for a splinter of a second, their eyes met, and a flood of warmth poured through Lexa's whole body as he nodded to her. But despite his reassurance, she knew she wasn't safe. Neither of them was.

Neri's tentacle wrapped around Lexa's torso once more, and she filled her lungs with air before getting pulled under.

Jinko swam back down with Ryke holding on to his fin. But as she sunk deeper into the darkness, they vanished from sight, and Lexa wondered if this was what dying felt like. Her burning chest grew light, and she tingled from head to toe.

Neri let out a terrible scream that made the ocean floor tremble. Her glowing eyes shone on Ryke, who had jumped from Jinko and buried his hook into Neri's shoulder. He yanked it out, tearing the flesh from her bones, and they became shrouded in a crimson wave of blood.

Lexa tried wiggling out of Neri's grip, but the more she moved, the more tightly it squeezed her. She pressed her lips shut, willing whatever was left of her oxygen not to escape. Neri's shrieks were drowned out by the loud thump of her heartbeat, slowing in rhythm.

Suddenly, the water cleared enough for Lexa to see Neri and Ryke in battle, the necklace dangling from her wrist. He tried to grab it, but Neri struck him with a tight fist in the gut. He lurched forward while Jinko slapped Neri with his tail.

Not that it did anything but mildly irritate her. But instead of reaching for Jinko, a second tentacle curled around Lexa, and there was simply nothing left in her body to give.

Through Neri's purple eyes, Lexa saw Ryke

slashing Neri's forearm with his hook, and though Neri cried out, her grip on Lexa never wavered. Instead, she dragged her farther down to the ocean floor. Lexa's body tingled as some sort of deadly farewell, and her eyes began to roll back.

Ryke seemed to have been growing tired as bubbles escaped his nose and he choked on the water. Lexa's heart burned. Drowning was torture enough, but watching Ryke die along with her was a fate worse than death. If she could speak, she would demand that he swim away and save himself. She hated Neri for putting her through this agony.

Another tentacle whipped at Ryke and struck him over his wound. The blow sent a mass of bubbles out of Ryke's mouth, and he jerked back on the ocean floor like a rock.

Lexa shut her eyes and waited for the darkness to come. She used the last of her consciousness to reach out in thought to anyone who might be able to hear. Then uttered her last words in case she didn't make it. *I'm sorry I failed you, Father.*

Seconds passed, but darkness did not come. Lexa opened her eyes, realizing that the heaviness in her limbs had evaporated. She floated upward, her body buzzing with energy and strength. And the cool salty taste of water was pleasant to swallow once more.

She looked up and met Neri's look of shock. Then she looked over to see Ryke unconscious and the pedant smashed into pieces floating above his hook.

Lexa hitched a breath.

Jinko bleated, slapping Neri across the cheek. Neri released her hold on Lexa just enough for her to wriggle away. She swam over to Ryke as Jinko and other fish blocked Neri from reaching after her.

Ryke looked peaceful. As though he was merely having a pleasant dream. But when Lexa pulled him upward, he was heavy and lifeless, like he was made of stone.

Jinko, take Ryke back to the beach.

Jinko did not hesitate, and within seconds, he had Ryke zooming up toward the shore.

Lexa turned back to Neri, and their eyes met. A thunderous growl vibrated the ocean, scattering the fish, and the ground began to shake as though a volcano was about to erupt.

So, this is how you want it to be? Neri said darkly.

Fine. I've tried to keep things clean, but now you will face my wrath.

Lexa pulled her heavy dress over her head and scowled at Neri, balling her hands into fists. *You don't scare me, sea monster. Do your worst.*

Neri laughed wickedly. *Monster, you say? Very well...*

Neri's tentacles jerked in awkward angles as they began to grow in size, and the skin on her torso ripped away, like it had merely been a disguise. Lexa watched in horror as Neri transformed into the most horrendous creature she had ever seen.

Though she still had the upper body of a mermaid, her skin was like that of a lizard, covered in shiny green scales. Her eyes grew black, and as she opened her mouth with a hissing roar, teeth like daggers glinted at her.

What are you? Lexa hissed, repulsed at the sight of the creature. *My father should have killed you a long time ago.*

After all, it was because of that wretched creature that Lexa grew up without a mother.

Neri howled with menacing laughter. *Did your precious daddy, Poseidon, ever tell you why you grew up without a mother?*

Lexa scowled. Neri had no right to invade her thoughts, and she certainly had no right to talk about her parents with such dishonor. She dug her fingernails into her palms. *You killed my mother! And for that, I will kill you. A life for a life.*

Neri let out a bubble of laughter, like Lexa had told the most delightful joke at a dinner party. Her reaction only riled Lexa up even more.

A life for life isn't about killing, it's about sacrificing your life for someone else. Which brings me to the truth about your mother. Neri grinned, looking utterly pleased with herself. *You want to know the truth, Princess?*

Her question sent a chill down Lexa's spine. She watched Neri slink forward, her tentacles waving in the water, playful but deadly. Lexa knew that just one strike could be a death blow.

You were born with very little life remaining in you, little mermaid. Your mother came to me for a cure. She gave her voice so that you could live. That was a life for a life. So, if you want to point fingers, look in the mirror for the person responsible for her death.

Lexa's mouth dropped open while her brain went into some sort of shock. *No...* She backed away from Neri's face. But Neri edged closer, her grin widening even more.

Yes, my naive Lexa. You killed your mother.

Lexa stopped, and her arms froze in place at her sides. A sense of cold dread flooded her senses. *I didn't… I wasn't… No!*

Neri cackled. *Like mother, like daughter. Defeated by me.*

The words hit her louder than a call of a blue whale, sending Lexa's body into shock. Neri spun around, sending up the dust of the ground, spinning around her until she disappeared in a cyclone of sparkling sand.

Lexa swam back and squinted through the floating particles, but then the water cleared as a mermaid appeared. Long black flowing hair reached her narrow shoulders. A seafoam blue fin and two big emerald eyes.

Lexa hitched a breath, blinking with horror at the sight of her… mother.

In her castle in Atlantis, there were murals of Lexa's mother. The image of her was etched in Lexa's mind from the many nights she snuck out of bed to sit by the portraits and weep.

And now there she was. Bobbing in front of Lexa.

Poseidon couldn't even tell the difference.

Lexa jerked back in shock. Neri had transformed into her mother. *You lured my father into that trap! You were working with the pirates!*

Suddenly, Lexa remembered their earlier conversation, and it all began to make sense. *That's how you were set free from your captors. You promised to give them mermaids in return for your freedom. You have been running the mermaid auctions.*

Neri tried striking Lexa, but she dodged the blow. *You pretty mermaids think you rule the sea. And what about the rest of us? Are we not good enough for Poseidon's kingdom?*

Lexa wanted nothing more than to strike Neri back, but she was too stunned, unable to fight when Neri was in the shape of her mother. *And your solution was to start a mermaid auction?*

Neri smirked. *The mermaid auction was a mere cruel irony. You mermaids think you're so precious. So, why not put a literal price on it?*

Lexa scowled. *You really are a monster.*

Neri smacked Lexa across the face, then pulled out a brass clip from her hair and raised it above her head. As she threw her arm down, Lexa dashed aside and punched Neri in the ribs.

She grunted, but the pain only strengthened her as she grabbed Lexa's shoulder and forced her back down, pinning her to the ground.

Neri's dark hair flowed back, revealing the nasty wound on her shoulder where Ryke had buried his hook. Lexa bit her lip, telling herself that this was not her mother. Just a disguise. She scrambled around, patting the earth beneath her, as Neri raised the brass clip like a dagger once more.

Lexa's fingers met with a small, jagged piece of her broken pendant. She took a breath. *You are not my mother!* Before Neri's hand came down in full force, Lexa dug the sharp edge into Neri's jugular.

Her mother's emerald eyes stretched wide as a fresh pool of blood flooded the water. Neri dropped the hair clip, and Lexa watched as her body jerked violently.

Her mother's disguise vanished, and the monster was back. Her long tentacles withered like a dying plant. After a few ragged breaths, Neri floated back and fell to the ground, stone dead. Bubbles of red floated upward as she bled out.

The sight of Neri's lifeless body brought Lexa back to Ryke. And without hesitating, she hurried for the surface.

Upon finding a group congregating on the

edge of the beach, Lexa swam toward the shore. Peter and Wendy held Tinkerbell in a glass dome while they clung to each other, while Ryke's crew knelt on the sand, sobbing and cursing into the wind.

"No…" she breathed, fear and dread washing over her.

Jinko joined her to offer a fin, and she took it because she was too stunned to move. All eyes were on her as she reached the shore, and a somber hush fell over the people. But Lexa didn't care to speak to any of them. She washed up on shore, wriggling forward. Without legs, she couldn't get to Ryke fast enough.

She reached for his cold body and immediately pumped his chest, making short breaths with each compression.

"Come back to me," she whispered, her voice hoarse.

"Lexa—"

She ignored Peter's gentle warning and continued to give Ryke chest compressions, willing his heart to start beating again. Her eyes blurred with tears as she pushed her entire weight onto his chest. She couldn't lose him. Not now. Not after everything they had overcome.

It was one thing to know she could never be with him, but the thought of a world without Ryke somewhere in it was unthinkable. He had to come back.

"Lexa, he's gone."

Someone's hands were on her shoulders, but she pushed them away, tears streaming down her face. "No!"

She went back to pumping his chest, but as minutes passed by and her attempts were futile, a terrible ache spread through Lexa's arms and gripped her heart in a vice.

She looked around the blurred figures around her, then at the quiet sea rolling to a yellow horizon, and she could not believe a new day would begin without Ryke in it.

"He can't be gone. I can't..." Lexa's words caught in her throat. More tears pricked her eyes. Her arm tickled, and she looked down at the forlorn face of Bob, sitting on her arm.

Oh, Princess.

Wendy buried her face in Peter's chest and began to cry.

"Princess Lexa?"

Lexa looked up to meet the Prince's devastated face. "Any obligations you had to my father are absolved with his death. And as newly appointed King of the Shores, I will ensure that no man will be permitted to hunt and enslave mermaids ever again. You have my word."

Lexa nodded but couldn't bring herself to care, feeling hollow inside.

She turned back to Ryke and lowered to press her forehead against his. He was gone, and the thought of a world without Ryke brought on unbearable pain. She couldn't live without him. She couldn't live in a world where he didn't exist. She just couldn't...

Then she remembered an old song she had once heard as a child. At Atlantis, there were whispers of a forbidden song. Her father had forbidden her to summon it, but what other choice did she have?

She pressed her forehead to Ryke's and whispered, "A life for a life, my love." Then, hoping she could remember the words, she began to sing.

"Morning sun of summer,
wake me from my slumber,
Flood my body with your rays."

Tears leaked out of Lexa's eyes as she sang the old song, and an icy chill washed over her skin like a cool breeze. Lexa could hear the gasps around her. She peeked to her left and saw thousands of mermaids bobbing in the water, watching. She kept her head pressed to Ryke's and shut her eyes.

"Lasting rays of moonlight,
Repair what has been damaged,
Bind these wounds with your shine."

Slowly, the air grew warm and a soft breeze encircled Lexa and Ryke as her singing grew louder and more exquisite than she'd ever known. To her wonderment, the mermaids joined in the song.

"Hades of the Underworld, hear my cry,
Bring back that which is owing, from your waters flowing.
Give one soul in exchange for mine."

The men stopped sobbing and looked in awe at the chorus of ethereal singing. The Prince sank to his knees and thrust a hand over his heart.

Lexa lifted her head and planted her hands on Ryke's unmoving chest, letting a flood of heat rush through her arms. She repeated the song with as much authority as she could muster, buoyed up by the chorus of voices from the sea.

"Morning sun of summer,
wake me from my slumber,
Flood my body with your rays.

Lasting rays of moonlight,
Repair what has been damaged,
Bind these wounds with your silver shine.
Return to me, that which is mine."

Lexa lowered her head and brushed her lips over Ryke's, and for the first time, something thumped against Lexa's palms. When it happened again, heat spread from Ryke's lips through his body, until he took in a gasp and opened his eyes.

Hardly daring to believe what she was seeing, Lexa's heart soared as Ryke's soft blue eyes blinked back at her. He panted as though he'd been running through the forest for an entire day, but then his eyes tilted with concern. "Why are you crying?" he asked, and his voice was the most beautiful sound Lexa had ever heard.

A golden light poured over them as the first rays of morning sun flooded the sky. Lexa placed her hands on Ryke's cheeks and beamed through happy tears. "You came back to me!"

Cheers surrounded the two lovers, but to Lexa, all she could look at was Ryke. She knew that their time together was short, for soon she would have to return to the sea until Hades came for her, and she wanted to soak up every last second. She only wished she could spend the rest of her days with Ryke, but he was alive, and they were together for that moment. That was enough for her. It had to be.

As though Ryke followed her thoughts, he wrapped her up in his arms and kissed her with as much passion as a tsunami engulfing the shore.

Lexa clung to Ryke's back, her heart splintering at the thought of being away from him. When they finally broke apart, Ryke glanced at her fin, his brows rising.

"You know what this means," Lexa said, dipping her head.

Ryke's expression hardened, and his jaw jutted out. He couldn't speak, but his slight nod said it all.

Lexa belonged in the sea. With Neri dead, and the necklace broken, there was no other way for Lexa to be human again. The two lovers stole more kisses, grasping each other and letting tears run freely as their time together ran out.

"Lexa."

They turned at the thunderous voice that came from the water. Poseidon floated among the mermaids, glowing yellow as though he was the very embodiment of sunshine. He raised his golden trident in the air. It glinted like a sword.

It was time to go home.

Lexa gave Ryke one final kiss and cupped his face. "I must go."

"I know," he said. "I wish things could be different."

They pressed their heads together and took a breath. Then Ryke cradled the back of Lexa's head and spoke softly into her ear with his cheek caressing hers. "You will always have my heart."

Lexa couldn't bear the pain any longer, she tore herself from his embrace, and with one last look at everyone's devastated faces, she threw herself off the beach and into the water.

She swam as fast as she could and flew into the outstretched arms of her father. She buried her face in his chest as he wrapped her up in a tight hug.

"Oh, Daddy!" She sobbed in his arms.

With a deep sigh, Poseidon tucked Lexa's hair away from her ear. "My precious Lexa, what did you do? You know Hades will be coming for you soon, and I have no power to stop him."

Lexa lifted her head and glanced at the beach. Ryke was still looking in her direction, immobile. Then she turned back to her father. "I know, but I love him, Daddy. I love him more than anything in this world."

Her father watched her for a long moment, then nodded slowly. "Well, I may not be able to stop Hades from taking you, but I can help you make the most of your final days in this world." He lifted his trident. "Is this what you really want?"

Lexa glanced at the trident, then at her father, and held her breath. "Are you saying…?"

Poseidon nodded. "If it is the life that you want, I will make you human."

Lexa almost burst into tears as a rush of emotion erupted in her chest. All she could do was nod.

"Well, then. So be it." Poseidon swam back, then pointed his trident to the skies. A clash of lightning struck it, lighting it up like it was made of a thousand burning stars.

Then he directed the trident to Lexa, and a jolt of electricity shot through the water and into her body.

Immediately her fin split into two slender legs, and she wiggled her toes, buzzing with a thrill. Jinko bleated with excitement.

Look what I found! he said, bringing Lexa's dress

on his nose. She giggled and put it on, every part of her body trembling as if she had been reborn.

"Thank you, Daddy," she said, going in for another hug.

"I love you, my princess." Poseidon's eyes grew misty as he smoothed out her hair. "Now go. Go be with your true love."

Lexa held onto Jinko, and he guided her back to the shore. Ryke's eyes widened as she grew closer, and he ran into the water to meet her.

"How—?" he asked, but never got to finish the question before Lexa was in his arms again, planting kisses all over his face.

He kissed her back with delight, then scooped her up in his arms and spun her around with joyful glee. The two of them laughed and frolicked in the water, waving goodbye to the mermaids and Poseidon as, one by one, they disappeared into the sea.

Finally, they walked hand in hand back to the crowd of pale faces, all looking as though they'd seen a ghost.

"Gents," Ryke announced, and his crew stood to attention. "Get the ship ready and prepare to set sail."

The crew scrambled about while Lexa stole

another gentle kiss from Ryke. It sent a rush of tingles through her body.

But then a sense of urgency rose in her heart. "Ryke," she said softly. He ripped away from her to read her face.

"What's wrong?"

"There's something you must know."

He touched her arms as if to steady her. "You can tell me anything."

"The song I sang to bring you back to life... it's forbidden for a reason. It has dire consequences."

"What kind of consequences?" Ryke asked.

"A life for a life." She thought about her mother and the sacrifice she'd made. It warmed her heart that they had made the same decision for those they loved.

Ryke lifted her chin with his finger. "What does that mean?"

"I'm not entirely sure, except that... someone from the underworld will come to claim a soul."

"Hades?"

"Most likely."

Ryke wrapped her in a protective embrace. "No one will ever take you away from me," he assured her.

"If only that were enough."

He cupped her face and looked into her deep green eyes. "Love is more powerful than death, my love, and I will die a thousand deaths to save you. Now…" His lips curve into a smile. "Let's go plan our wedding."

EPILOGUE

*K*illian swam through the portal from the Underworld and rose up to a pool in a cave. He climbed out of the water, his boots thumping the stone ground as he shook water out of his hair and squared his shoulders, ready for a fight.

But surprisingly, he was alone.

He glanced up at the dancing reflections of the water on the cave ceiling, searching for the formidable sea monster, Neri.

He'd heard rumors that Neri was dead. Killian thought it was a joke, but now he could see it was true.

Relaxing, he strode through the cave and set his mind on the task at hand.

First, he needed a boat.

Outside, the salty sea breeze whipped through his hair, and a small fishing boat with two men was bobbing in the water not far off the shore. The corners of Killian's mouth lifted, and he rolled up his sleeves to reveal the bulging muscles on his forearms. Then he marched toward them.

*K*illian bathed in the golden sunshine as he leaned against the railing on one of the King of the Shores' royal ships. He had snuck in under the disguise of a servant. It was not easy finding someone his size to steal clothes from.

He stood a foot taller than any man on the boat, and his broad shoulders and arms were big enough to make even Hercules nervous.

He looked around the boat again, the music drawing him back to the party. A server walked by, and Killian picked up a glass of sparkling wine as he surveyed the small group surrounding a bride and groom.

He thought it was the oddest selection of

guests for a wedding. But then, it was an odd pairing. Never in all his years had he heard of a pirate marrying a mermaid. But here they were, making history.

A lobster sat in a prime position between the bride and groom, holding two sparkling rings in his pincers.

A seagull stood proudly to one side, wearing a black tie. And a dolphin watched from the other side of the boat with a top hat on its smooth head.

If Killian had not been so focused on his mission, he'd have cracked a smile. Maybe even made a sarcastic remark. But he needed to keep a low profile.

A sacrifice was called for. The Underworld was missing a soul, and it was his job to get it.

The happy couple exchanged vows, and the guests cheered as the two of them kissed. The seas were calm for the entire day, and thousands of mermaids bobbed in the waters near the ship, flooding the air with their sickly sweet tunes.

Men often whispered about the beautiful mermaid melodies and their deadly abilities, but the siren's trance had no power over Killian.

The sky turned crimson as the sun began to

set over the ice mountains. Only then did Killian step forward and show his true colors.

He knew that his eyes had flashed cyan blue because Lexa, the bride, looked at him like she was seeing a ghost. Then she muttered something to her new husband and kissed his cheek as they stopped dancing.

"I'll be right back," she whispered, but not too quiet that Killian could not hear it.

Lexa rushed through the crowd of dancers, grabbed Killian's arm, and pulled him aside, taking him to the darkest corner of the ship. When she turned, her green eyes shone like two emeralds, and her face had turned ashen white. The pretty pink color of her cheeks completely faded.

"Please, just let me have tonight," she said, her voice shaken. "Just one night."

Killian smirked. As if anyone could barter with a guard of the Underworld.

"Don't worry, Princess, I'm not here for you," he said before taking a long swig of his drink. The bubbles tickled all the way down. He had missed human wine. It had so much more flavor than the grim drinks he had back home.

Lexa's eyes stretched wide. "But I sang the forbidden song, I made an oath…"

Killian raised a thick brow and surveyed the mermaid's look of disbelief. Lines had appeared on the corners of her eyes, and he wondered if she had gotten any sleep since she had summoned him.

"Let me explain a few rules of the Underworld…" He tucked a strand of hair behind her ear, but she shrugged away like she'd been zapped by an electric eel. Undeterred, Killian set his drink down. "You summoned your beloved pirate's soul back from the Underworld…"

"Yes, I know but—"

Killian raised both eyebrows and gave her a firm look. She stopped and shut her mouth.

"As you are aware, the Underworld delivered. But now we need something in return," he explained, keeping his eyes on Lexa.

She swallowed loudly. "And I'm ready to go, but not tonight. Please, can we wait until morning? Just give me one night with my husband—"

"You're not listening, are you, Princess?" He leaned forward and sniffed her, his nostrils picked up the sickly sweet scent. And the sound of her racing heart thumped against his ears as though it was his own. "I can't take you to the Underworld. You have too much life in you."

Lexa took a step back, pinching her brows and looking at Killian like he'd said a bad word. "But you said you need…"

"A life for a life, that is correct," Killian confirmed, standing tall again. He smiled, but Lexa looked more terrified than ever, then her eyes flew in all directions, looking at the happy people dancing on the ship.

"If you're not here for me… who are you here for?" Her words barely came out in a whisper, but Killian heard them nonetheless. He took a big breath of the sea air, and all manner of scents mingled together, flooding him with information.

He could sense the emotions of every person on the ship. And of them all, there was one that had a delicious scent. One that made him burn inside.

"I can only take a soul that has given up the will to live, one so tormented by life that they will gladly surrender."

"So, you're not taking me to the Underworld?" she asked in disbelief. "I can live out my life with Ryke?"

"Correct."

Lexa's frown deepened. "Who will you be taking then?"

Killian inclined his head with a gruff laugh. "Go and please your husband. Enjoy your life together. I have no business with you."

Reluctantly, Lexa ran back to the arms of her groom, who started to dance with her again. Then the crowd parted, and a figure with the darkest aura met his eyes.

Killian strode across the ship, never taking his eyes off the woman, delighting in the sweet, addicting scent of guilt and hopelessness.

He stopped with less than a foot from her. A pair of pretty blue eyes blinked up at him, framed with golden hair that fell in soft waves below her shoulders. She wore a pale blue gown with a tight corset, giving him an eyeful of her pert bosom.

"May I have this dance?" He held out his hand, and when she placed hers into it, he marveled at how tiny she was compared to him. Her feeble body was so delicate, it was like dancing with a doll.

The blonde maiden was a skillful dancer, not once did she stumble or step on his feet. And all the while, she held his gaze, her plump lips spread open to form a perfect 'o.'

"To whom do I owe this honor of a dance?" she asked, her voice prettier than any of the thousands of mermaids.

Killian firmed his grip on her waist and led the dance, holding her slender body pressed up against him. The closer he got, the stronger the scent of her was, and it had him more intoxicated than drinking a gallon of beer. "The name is Killian," he said, dipping her as she arched her back. His mouth hovered mere inches from hers, and he couldn't help but notice the swell of her chest heaving under his gaze.

"I'm Ella," she said between breaths.

Killian lifted her up and spun her around before setting her down to continue their dance. By now, the dancers had moved away to give them room, and some people stood by and watched. But Killian paid them no attention. Ella was all he had eyes for. Her scent, her body, her sweet, tormented soul was his for the taking. And he was ready for it.

"I know all about you, Ella," he said in a low tone. Her eyes flashed at him.

"What, what do you mean?" she asked, batting her lashes. Killian smirked and twirled her on the spot before he pulled her in again.

"I know what you did to the King. I know you're wracked with guilt over it, too…"

"I, I am not."

"Don't lie to me, Ella. I can sense it on you."

"You can sense guilt?"

"Yes, and you reek of it."

Ella stiffened in his grasp, but Killian did not let her go.

"What do you want from me?" Ella asked, her voice tight. Killian sensed a flash of defiance behind her eyes.

He smirked again, then leaned forward and whispered into her ear while she trembled in his arms. "I want your soul. I've come to take you to the Underworld."

Ella pulled back to look at him with horror, then she drove her knee into his groin.

He bent over in pain, and she ripped herself from his arms. "Stay away from me," she huffed, then turned on her heels and fled through the crowd of dancers.

Once the blinding pain faded and Killian could follow, he saw her running down the wooden ramp docked on the sandy beach, and a small-heeled shoe lay on the deck by the wooden plank.

Killian picked it up and chuckled as he looked out at the tiny flowy dress disappearing into the night. He thought it extremely amusing that Ella thought she could hide from him.

*R*ead Ella's story in book 6 of the Fairytales Reimagined series, Heart of Glass. Get your copy here.

A note from the authors: Thank you so much for reading out swashbuckling story! If you loved it, we'd really appreciate a nice review and share the series with your friends! See you in the next book!

Made in United States
Orlando, FL
13 October 2023

37839418R00169